David Malouf was born in Brisbane; his father's family came from Lebanon and his mother's family from London. He was educated at the Brisbane Grammar School and the University of Queensland, where he taught for two years. He went to England in 1959 and for nearly ten years taught in London and Birkenhead. He then returned to Australia and was appointed a senior tutor and later a lecturer at Sydney University. He now lives in Italy.

He has published four collections of poetry, 'Interiors' in *Four Poets*, *Bicycle and other poems*, *Neighbours in a Thicket*, and *Poem, 1975–76*. *Neighbours in a Thicket* won him the Grace Leven Prize for poetry, the James Cook Award for the best Australian book of 1974 and the gold medal of the Australian Literature Society. His first novel, *Johnno*, was published in 1975 in Australia. *An Imaginary Life* won the New South Wales Premier's Literary Award for fiction in 1979.

AN
IMAGINARY
LIFE

A NOVEL BY

David Malouf

PUBLISHED BY PAN BOOKS

First published 1978 by Chatto & Windus Limited
This Picador edition published 1980 by Pan Books
(Australia) Pty Limited
68 Moncur Street, Woollahra, New South Wales
Reprinted 1982

© David Malouf 1978
ISBN 0 330 27004 4

National Library of Australia
Cataloguing-in-Publication data
Malouf, David, 1934–
    An imaginary life
    First published, London: Chatto & Windus, 1978
    I. Title
A823'.3

Printed and bound in Australia by
The Dominion Press

To Christopher

An Imaginary Life

WHEN I first saw the child I cannot say. I see myself—I might be three or four years old—playing under the olives at the edge of our farm, just within call of the goatherd, and I am talking to the child, whether for the first time or not I cannot tell at this distance. The goatherd is dozing against an olive bole, his head rolled back to show the dark line of his jaw and the sinews of his scraggy neck, the black mouth gaping. Bees shift amongst the herbs. The air glitters. It must be late summer. There are windblown poppies in the grass. A black he-goat is up on his hind legs reaching for vineshoots.

The child is there. I am three or four years old. It is late summer. It is spring. I am six. I am eight. The child is always the same age. We speak to one another, but in a tongue of our own devising. My brother, who is a year older, does not see him, even when he moves close between us.

He is a wild boy.

I have heard the goatherds speak of a wild boy, whether this one or another I do not know; and of course I do not admit to them, or to anyone, that I know him. The wild boy they speak of lives among wolves, in the ravines to the east, beyond the cultivated farms and villas of our well-watered valley.

There really are wolves out there. I have heard stories of how they

9

raid the outlying pastures, and once I think I heard one howling in the snow. Unless it was the child. And I have seen a wolf's head that one of the hunters brought back to hang up as a warning in his fold. It was gray, and not very fierce looking, despite the curling back of the flesh over its fanged jaw. I thought of the child, and how wolves must have something in their nature which is kindly, and which connects with our kind, or how else could the child live amongst them? What was frightening was the way the head had been hacked off, with ropes of dark blood hanging from it and the fur at its throat matted with blood. Later I heard, again from the goatherds perhaps, that there is indeed some part of our nature that we share with wolves, and something of their nature that is in us, since there are men, at certain phases of the moon, who can transform themselves into wolves. They close their human mind like a fist and when they open it again it is a wolf's paw. The skull bulges, the jaw pushes out to become a snout. Hair prickles down their spine, grows rough on their belly. The body slouches and is on all fours. The voice thickens. It is the moon draws them on. I believed such things in those days, and wondered. Was the child a wolf boy? Were those wolf men who lived secretly among us, changing themselves painfully at the moon's bidding, children who had been captured from the wilds and brought in among us, to be adapted to the ways of men?

Sometime when my own body began to change and I discovered the first signs of manhood upon me, the child left and did not reappear, though I dreamt of him often enough in those early years, and have done so since. I have forgotten the language we used, and if he were to reappear, perhaps we could no longer communicate. Did he have some message for me then? If so, he failed to deliver it. Or did so and it has slipped my mind. Or the language he used on whatever occasion it was had already passed my understanding and could not be translated into daily speech. I believe (I think I have *always believed) that he will come again. But in what guise? As a child still? As a man of my own age? As a wolf? Or has he the power to adopt other forms as well? Has he already returned to me, perhaps, in a form so humble, so ordinary, that I failed to perceive his presence?*

I tell no one of this, as all those years ago I was careful to admit to no one that he was there—not even my brother who was the same age and would have understood. Under all my skepticism this grain of belief.

I

IT is the desolateness of this place that day after day fills my mind with its perspectives. A line of cliffs, oblique against the sky, and the sea leaden beyond. To the west and south, mountains, heaped under cloud. To the north, beyond the marshy river mouth, empty grasslands, rolling level to the pole.

For eight months of the year the world freezes. Some polar curse is breathed upon the land. It whitens overnight. Then when the ice loosens at last, and breaks up, the whole plain turns muddy and stinks, the insects swarm and plague us, hot mists steam amongst the tussocks. I have found no tree here that rises amongst the low, grayish brown scrub. No flower. No fruit. We are at the ends of the earth. Even the higher orders of the vegetable kingdom have not yet arrived among us. We are centuries from the notion of an orchard or a garden made simply to please. The country lies open on every side, walled in to the west and south, level to the north and to the northeast, with a view to infinity. The sharp incline of the cliffs leads to sky. The river flats, the wormwood scrubs, the grasslands beyond, all lead to a sky that hangs close above us, heavy with snow, or is empty as far as the eye can see or the mind imagine, cloudless, without wings.

But I am describing a state of mind, no place.

I am in exile here.

The village called Tomis consists of a hundred huts made of woven branches and mud, with roofs of thatch and floors of beaten mud covered with rushes. Each hut has a walled yard, and a byre where the animals can be brought in and stalled for the winter. Above the byre, in one large room, we sleep and eat in the winter, on wooden benches above a layer of slow-burning peat. In summer the rest of the house is opened up and I have a room of my own, with a low table for writing and a palliasse of clean straw.

My life here has been stripped to the simplest terms. I live with the headman of the village, who has been set to watch over me, and maybe, when the time comes, to finish me off. The household consists of the headman, his mother (an old woman of nearly eighty) and his daughter-in-law and her child. They are rough, kindly people, and the old man, for all that he is a barbarian, treats me with some regard for my former position. If anything, I am ignored, left to my own devices, to wander about the village or as far as it is safe to go into the fields. They have no need to fear my escape. In all the known world, where the emperor rules, I have no official existence. And beyond this last outpost is the unknown. Even supposing I had the energy for it in my present condition, where could I go?

I move around the muddy little fort, or I make excursions into the scrub, though never beyond sight of the walls, since at any season the village may be attacked by the savages who inhabit the open grasslands to the north and who periodically come howling in packs to steal our animals or fire the outlying fields. The whole village is an armed camp. And I am the least person here —a crazy, comic old man, grotesque, tearful, who understands nothing, can say nothing, and whose ways, so it must seem to these dour people, are absurdly out of keeping with the facts of our daily existence. They feed me. They provide a corner where I can sleep. They are not uncivil. But no one in Tomis speaks my tongue, and for nearly a year now I have heard no word of my own language; I am rendered dumb. I communicate like a child with grunts and signs, I point, I raise my eyebrows, questioning, I burst into tears of joy if someone —a child even—understands what I am trying to say. In the open I go about shouting, talking to myself simply to keep the words in my head, or to drive them out of it. My days in this place, my nights, are terrible beyond description. All day I wander in a dream, as isolated from the world of men as if I belonged to another species. At night I discover in sleep what the simple daylight blinds me to: that the dark side of every object here, and even more, the landscape itself when night shadows flow over it, is a vast page whose tongue I am unable to decipher, whose message to me I am unable to interpret. In dream after dream I venture out beyond the stubbled fields into the desolate plain beyond, into the grasslands beyond the edge of our world. The wind rolls over them. They heave like the sea, hissing, sighing, and the air is filled with the wings of cabbage moths. I fall to my knees and begin digging with my long nails in the earth. Sometimes wolves come, and they claw at the earth beside me. Howling. We dig together, and they pay no more attention to me than they would to a ghost. But I know that whatever it is they are scratching after, I must discover before them, or I am lost. So I dig harder, faster, sweating, with the moonlight greasy upon me. Unable to tell myself: this is a dream.

I know what it is we are looking for. It is the grave of the poet Ovid—Publius Ovidius Naso, Roman of the equestrian order, poet. In all this desolation, no one knows where he lies.

Called Naso because of the nose.

I speak to you, reader, as one who lives in another century, since this is the letter I will never send. It is addressed neither to my wife nor to my lawyer at Rome, nor even to the emperor; but to you, unknown friend, who do not exist at this time of my writing and whose face, whose form even, I cannot imagine. Can one imagine the face of a god? For that surely is what you must be at your great distance from us—the god who has begun to stir in our depths, to gather his being out of us, and will, at the other end of the great cycle that has already rocked our world with its quakings, have evolved at last and come into being.

I cast this letter upon the centuries, uncertain in what landscape of unfamiliar objects it may come to light, and with what eyes you will read it. Is Latin still known to you? I bury it deep in the ice, in one of the tumulus graves whose rocks are sealed with ice that never melts and where no one from our Roman world has ever ventured. Only after a thousand years, when the empire has fallen and no longer has the power of silence over us, will this letter come safely to your hands. I am the poet Ovid—born on the cusp between two houses of the zodiac, where the Fishes, tugging in their opposite directions, plunge below the horizon, and the Ram ascends; between two cycles of time, the millenium of the old gods, that shudders to its end, and a new era that will come to its crisis at some far point in the future I can barely conceive of, and where you, reader, sit in a lighted room whose furnishings I do not recognize, or in the late light of a garden whose blooms I do not know, translating this—with what difficulty?—into your own tongue.

Have you heard my name? Ovid? Am I still known? Has some line of my writing escaped the banning of my books from all the libraries and their public burning, my expulsion from the Latin tongue? Has some secret admirer kept one of my poems and so preserved it, or committed it to memory? Do my lines still pass secretly somewhere from mouth to mouth? Has some phrase of mine slipped through as a quotation, unnoticed by the authorities, in another man's poem? Or in a letter? Or in a saying that has become part of common speech and cannot now be eradicated?

Have I survived?

I write this by candlelight. It is dark as night in this windowless room. Little spiders and other insects live in the thatched roofing and crawl about the floor, falling in your hair or in the bowl of soup you are eating, swarming in the folds of your garments. You get used to it after a while.

I had never had much contact with the creatures before this, not even with dogs or cats. Now I find something oddly companionable about them. Like me, they too cannot speak. They move about in the cracks, in the gaps in our lives, and are harmless. Even the spiders, poor creatures. Do they have a language of their own, I wonder? If so, I might try to learn it. As easy do that as master the barbarous guttural tongue my neighbors speak.

I have begun to recognize some sounds in it. But just to hear the old man shouting in the yard to his grandson, or muttering in the twilight to the young woman, comes close at times to maddening me; it is like trying to remember something you have forgotten, that glows at the very edge of your mind but refuses to reveal itself. I feel as cut off as one of those spiders. Or a rat balancing on a rafter and hearing the poets read. It is as if I had suddenly slipped back a step in the order of things, or been transformed, by a witch's curse, into one of the lower species. But of course it is no witch who has done this. No magic has been practiced against me. All that has been evoked is the power of the law. I have, by the working of the highest known authority, been cast out into what is indeed another order of beings, those who have not yet climbed up through a hole in their head and become fully human, who have not yet entered what we call society and become Romans under the law.

But they are, even so, of our species, these Getae. I listen to them talk. The sounds are barbarous, and my soul aches for the refinements of our Latin tongue, that perfect tongue in which all things can be spoken, even pronouncements of exile. I listen, and what moves me most is that I recognize the tunes. This one, I know, is tenderness; this regret, this anger, this an old man's tune for soothing a child who falls over, weeps, tells his ills, and must be led back to call the stone by names one might almost recognize out of one's most distant childhood: "Naughty, naughty stone!"

Meanwhile, there are the spiders. Could I tune my ears to their speech also? Since they too must communicate with one another. I might begin to write again in the spiders' language. *The New Metamorphoses of the poet Ovid in his Exile, in the spiders' tongue.*

Sometimes, wandering aimlessly about, I stop to watch the women at work in the courtyard, sorting and grinding grain, and one of them will look up and scowl, or smile, out of some world of her own that I cannot touch. There are many seeds: gold, greenish yellow, brown, blue. I guess what some of them may be, but do not recall their names. I know the names of seeds, of course, from having used them for the beauty of the sound itself in poems I have written: coriander, cardamom. But I have no idea what any but the commonest of them look like. Once or twice I have taken one of the seeds on my forefinger and placed it on my palm, while the puzzled women looked on. On one occasion the youngest of them laughed and said a word: *Korschka.* I looked at the seed and she nodded, as if I were a child, and said again, rounding her lips in an exaggerated fashion, *Kors-chka!*, then took one of the seeds on her tongue and bit through it. I did the same, but failed to recognize the taste. In isolation, and without the hundred other herbs and spices that might have gone with it in our Roman cookery, it brought no shock of recognition to my palate and no name to my mind. So I know the word for this seed now, and its taste, and its shape and color, but cannot translate it back into my own experience.

Must it all be like this from now on? Will I have to learn everything all over again like a child? Discovering the world as a small child does, through the senses, but with all things deprived of the special magic of their names in my own tongue?

There is nothing to be said of our village except that it has a hundred or so huts. The narrow streets between them are of mud. A few pigs wallow in it, or a few dirty geese, and the mud is compounded of one part earth and nine parts the trodden mess of these creatures over what must be a thousand generations. Naked children come out after the rain to sit in pools with the geese, or they chase the pigs between the houses, their squeals and the squealing of the piglets, to my ears, indistinguishable. Beyond the walls of the stockade are a few patches of grain, which the women gather and pound, and among the stalks grow herbs and other plants whose seeds have to be separated by hand from the wheat, the wild oats and the barley. They have no other form of cultivation.

It is midsummer now. The river flats steam and hum

with midges. But in a few weeks the first of the winter will be upon us. The north winds blow in across the river, out of the Scythian steppes, laying the reeds flat, whipping up the water. Already the men are out cutting slabs of peat, which they will lay up in piles against the cold. The women are stocking the garners with grain and smoking sides of pork they hang beneath the rafters. Once the river freezes we must stay in the stockade day and night, and day and night men will keep guard. The river now is our protection. But two months from now it will become a bridge of ice and the hordes from the north will come pouring across it, plundering, raping, burning. My people here are only relatively savage. The real barbarians I have yet to see. I have only dreamt of them.

I dreamt, one night lately, that I walked out in the moonlight, down the street between the huts, hearing the little pigs grunting behind me, singing of their sucked bones, and out into the strange light of the marshes. The moon rode high over the reeds, its face halved by a line of cloud like a lidded eye—my own eye, half-waking, and open like an owl's eye, half-closed on the dark.

I walked on the river, which swirled like smoke under me, and I was moonlight. I came to the further bank. A vast plain stretched away, flat, flat, featureless, it was all dust, swirling beneath me, and out of the dust no creature stirred, not a serpent even. It was original.

Suddenly, not out of the dust of the plain but out of the swirling sky, a horde of forms came thundering towards me—men, yes, horses, yes, and I thought of what I do not believe in and know belongs only to our world of fables, which is where I found myself: the centaurs. But these were not the tamed creatures of our pastoral myths. They were gigantic, and their power, the breath of their nostrils, the crash of their hooves, the rippling light of their flanks, was terrible. These, I knew, were gods.

In whom I also do not believe.

I stood silent in the center of the plain and they began to wheel in great circles about me, uttering cries —not of malice, I thought, but of mourning. *Let us into your world,* they seemed to be saying. *Let us cross the river into your empire. Let us into your lives. Believe in us. Believe.*

Slowly they came to a halt.

Stood.

Breathing.

There was a silence, vast as the plain, and I heard my own heartbeats, like the faintest echo of their hooves, and my own breathing like theirs, only closer, tearing at my chest. And one of those creatures, out of the shadowy forces that blocked out the whole horizon above me, came slowly, putting its hooves down gently in the dust, towards me, and halted just a foot away, so that I felt its breath, its warmth, and thought I heard on the flow of its breath a sound whose syllables I could interpret. Once again, it was the tune that I recognized. As if, having no language of my own now, I had begun to listen for another meaning.

I put out my hand, touched it.

And something came out of the depths of my sleep towards the point where we stood facing one another, like a reflection rising to the surface of a mirror. It was there, outside me, a stranger. And something in me that

24

Elise Marcaux, Melbourne

was its reflection had come up to meet it.

I woke, cried out. And the word I uttered was not in my own tongue.

I have tried since to remember that word, but the sound has sunk back into my sleep. If I could recall that sound, and speak the word again, I think I would know what it is I have named, what it is that I have encountered. What it is out there that is waiting to receive me.

Called Naso because of the nose.

What my ancestor had a nose for I do not know. What I had a nose for was news—what was fashionable, what would go.

I am essentially a social creature. Some poets, Vergil for example, have an ear, perfect in every way. I have a nose. And noses are political, even when all you are putting them into are the most private places. Perhaps most political just then. Noses get you into trouble. I could sniff out too well what everyone wants to hear, has begun to think, and *will* think too, once I have said it.

After a century of war in which whole families had destroyed one another in the name of patriotism, we were at peace. I stepped right into it—an age of soft self-indulgent muddle, of sophisticated impudence, when we all seemed to have broken out of bounds at last into an enlightenment so great that there was no longer any need for belief.

"The gods are not quite dead" was my news from the universe, "since their names are on all our lips—not to mention the monuments to them that are dedicated daily by our beloved leader. But they too have ceased to be serious. They have entered the age of play. They have abandoned the holy places and taken up residence in fables that require only our amused detachment from disbelief. They would be embarrassed by anything so glum and humorless as our grandfathers' piety. We are free at last to believe in *ourselves*. Since there are no rules, we must make some. Let them be absurd! Since there are no more restrictions, we invent them. May they be perverse! . . ." And so on, in the same vein.

I was discovering for my generation a new national style. No more civic virtues—since we all know where they lead. No more patriotism. No more glorification of men at arms. No more guides in verse to bee keeping and sheep drench and the loves of shepherd boys with a taste for Greek. My world was strictly personal, a guide, in good plain terms, to such country matters as can be explored in the two square meters of a bed.

The emperor has created his age. It is called Augustan, as our historians, with their eye fixed firmly on the present, have already announced. It is solemn, orderly, monumental, dull. It exists in the eulogies that are made for him (to which I decline to contribute) and in marble that will last forever.

I too have created an age. It is coterminous with his, and has its existence in the lives and loves of his subjects. It is gay, anarchic, ephemeral and it is fun. He hates me for it.

Of course in the short run Augustus wins. And the short run is now. I have been relegated—that is our nice word for it—to the limits of the known world, and expelled from the confines of our Latin tongue.

But in the shadow of a portico dedicated by his sister to her faithful husband, someone tonight is being fucked; because in a poem once I made it happen, and made that particular act, in that particular place, a gesture of public defiance. Each night now Augustus thinks of it and bites his thumb. There are places closer than the Black Sea where the emperor's power stops. The Portico of Marcellus is one of them.

But I am here, and all this, all of it, is far behind me. How foolish it now seems, my irony, my little impieties, my dancing on the tightrope over the abyss. I have smelled my way to the very edge of things, where Nothing begins. That's where a Nose gets you. I sniff and sniff and there is no news from out there, and no news from in here either. I am dead. I am relegated to the region of silence. All I can do is shout.

And that is what I am doing.

I walk up and down the stony shoreline under the cliffs, whose shadow divides the shingle into distinct segments of light and dark. I walk among the fishermen, shouting—watching them haul in their glittering surprises, their nameless catch, from out of the sea. Or I stride about in the brushwood on the cliff tops, flapping my arms against the cold, watching storms push up black out of nowhere, or great streams of thistledown and flock travelling white on the wind, and I launch my shouts.

It's a long way to Rome. If they are ever to hear me again I must raise my voice and let these torrents of dark air that flow west over the plains carry me with them. I have been silenced. But will not be stilled.

27

How can I give you any notion—you who know only landscapes that have been shaped for centuries to the idea we all carry in our souls of that ideal scene against which our lives should be played out—of what earth was in its original bleakness, before we brought to it the order of industry, the terraces, fields, orchards, pastures, the irrigated gardens of the world we are making in our own image.

Do you think of Italy—or whatever land it is you now inhabit—as a place given you by the gods, ready-made in all its placid beauty? It is not. It is a created place. If the gods are with you there, glowing out of a tree in some pasture or shaking their spirit over the pebbles of a brook in clear sunlight, in wells, in springs, in a stone that marks the edge of your legal right over a hillside; if the gods are there, it is because you have discovered them there, drawn them up out of your soul's need for them and dreamed them into the landscape to make it shine. They are with you, sure enough. Embrace the tree trunk and feel the spirit flow back into you, feel the warmth of the stone enter your body, lower yourself into the spring as into some liquid place of your body's other life in sleep. But the spirits have to be recognized to become real. They are not outside us, nor even entirely within, but flow back and forth between us and the objects we have made, the landscape we have shaped and move in. We have dreamed all these things in our deepest lives and they are ourselves. It is our self we are making out there, and when the landscape is complete we shall have become the gods who are intended to fill it.

It is as if each creature had the power to dream itself

out of one existence into a new one, a step higher on the ladder of things. Having conceived in our sleep the idea of a further being, our bodies find, slowly, painfully, the physical process that will allow them to break their own bonds and leap up to it. So that the stone sleeping in the sun has once been molten fire and became stone when the fire was able to say, in its liquid form: "I would be solid, I would be stone"; and the stone dreams now that the veins of ore in its nature might become liquid again and move, but within its shape as stone, so that slowly, through long centuries of aching for such a condition, for softness, for a pulse, it feels one day that the transformation has begun to occur; the veins loosen and flow, the clay relaxes, the stone, through long ages of imagining some further life, discovers eyes, a mouth, legs to leap with, and is toad. And the toad in turn conceives the possibility, now that it can move over the earth, of taking to the air, and slowly, without ever ceasing to be toad, dreams itself aloft on wings. Our bodies are not final. We are moving, all of us, in our common humankind, through the forms we love so deeply in one another, to what our hands have already touched in lovemaking and our bodies strain towards in each other's darkness. Slowly, and with pain, over centuries, we each move an infinitesimal space towards it. We are creating the lineaments of some final man, for whose delight we have prepared a landscape, and who can only be god.

I have seen the end of all this, clearly, in imagination: the earth transfigured and the gods walking upon it in their bodies' light. And I have seen the earth, as you have reader, already prepared for it, since our minds can conceive, our hands fashion, what we are not yet ready to enter: cornfields a fathom high, stacked in the sunlight, swaying under the moon; olive groves blowing from green to silver in a breeze, as if some god spoke the word *silver,* and his breath in passing over the scene transformed it with the turning of the leaves. You know all this. It is the earth as we have made it, clearing, grafting, transplanting, carrying seeds from one place to another, following no plan that we could enunciate, but allowing our bellies to lead us, and some other, deeper hunger, till the landscape we have made reveals to us the creatures we long for and must become.

I know how far we have come because I have been back to the beginnings. I have seen the unmade earth. It is flat and featureless, swamp in summer, a frozen waste in winter, without a tree or a flower or a made field, and only the wildest seeds growing together in their stunted clumps or blowing about at random on the breeze. It is a place of utter desolation, the beginning. I know it like the inside of my head. You can have no idea how far we have come, or how far back I have been to see all this; how rudimentary our life is in its beginnings.

And yet even here there are stirrings of new life. The first seeds are there to be separated and nurtured, and led on their long path to perfection.

Out walking today in my old sandals and cloak, with a straw hat to keep off the sun, stumbling about talking to myself in the muddy waste towards the river, I was stopped in my tracks by a little puff of scarlet amongst the wild corn.

Scarlet!

It is the first color I have seen in months. Or so it seems. Scarlet. A little wild poppy, of a red so sudden it made my blood stop. I kept saying the word over and over to myself, scarlet, as if the word, like the color, had escaped me till now, and just saying it would keep the little windblown flower in sight. Poppy. The magic of saying the word made my skin prickle, the saying almost a greater miracle than the seeing. I was drunk with joy. I danced. I shouted. Imagine the astonishment of my friends at Rome to see our cynical metropolitan poet, who barely knows a flower or a tree, dancing about in broken sandals on the earth, which is baked hard and cracked in some places, and in others puddled with foul-smelling mud—to see him dancing and singing to himself in celebration of this bloom. Poppy, scarlet poppy, flower of my far-off childhood and the cornfields round our farm at Sulmo, I have brought you into being again, I have raised you out of my earliest memories, out of my blood, to set you blowing in the wind. Scarlet. Magic word on the tongue to flash again on the eye. Scarlet. And with it all the other colors come flooding back, as magic syllables, and the earth explodes with them, they flash about me. I am making the spring. With yellow of the ox-eyed daisy of our weedy olive groves, with blue of cornflower, orange of marigold, purple of foxglove, even the pinks and cyclamens of my mother's garden that I have forgotten all these years. They come back . . . though there was, in fact, just a single poppy, a few blown petals of a tissue fineness and brightness, round the crown of seeds.

Where had it come from? I searched and searched but

could find no other. The seeds must have blown in and taken root. But from where? From the sea—carried high up in a stream of luminous dust and let fall among us. Or in the entrails of some bird on its way north, and growing out of the bird's casual droppings as it passed.

I sit on the ground and observe it. I love this poppy. I shall watch over it.

Suddenly my head is full of flowers of all kinds. They sprout out of the earth in deep fields and roll away in my skull. I have only to name the flowers, without even knowing what they look like, the color, the shape, the number of petals, and they burst into bud, they click open, they spread their fragrance in my mind, opening out of the secret syllables as I place them like seeds upon my tongue and give them breath. I shall make whole gardens like this. I am Flora. I am Persephone. I have the trick of it now. All it needs is belief.

And this, as I might have guessed, is how it is done. We give the gods a name and they quicken in us, they rise in their glory and power and majesty out of minds, they move forth to act in the world beyond, changing us and it. So it is that the beings we are in process of becoming will be drawn out of us. We have only to find the name and let its illumination fill us. Beginning, as always, with what is simple.

Poppy, you have saved me, you have recovered the earth for me. I know how to work the spring.

It is about to begin. All my life till now has been wasted. I had to enter the silence to find a password that would release me from my own life.

And yet the words were already written. I wrote

them years ago, and only now discover what they meant, what message they had for me: "You will be separated from yourself and yet be alive."

Now I too must be transformed.

II

IT is almost evening. We sit, the old man, the child, his mother and myself, in the last warmth of the sun in the yard behind our wooden palisade.

It is bare, this yard, with benches, a rack where gourds hang from strings to dry in the sun, and laid out in a circle, the stones the women use for grinding. The old woman, the headman's mother, never joins us here. Instead she mutters about in the room behind, occasionally shoving her head, with its toothless jaw, through the little opening and telling us, I gather, how cold it is, and warning the younger woman that the boy should be wrapped up or in bed. Sometimes she just leans on one bony elbow and listens, startling us with her sudden laughter.

This is the quiet time of the day when the harder tasks are over, the hour before bed. Big clouds move fast overhead, and there is a wind blowing from the north, from the steppes, with the cold edge of the river upon it. Leaves go flying up in spirals above the fence poles. But out of the wind, in the late sunshine, it is warm.

We have eaten our supper out here: soup made out

of nettles, a goat's milk cheese flavored with herbs. The bowls are beside us on the earth. The young woman is at work again, sewing strips of rough hide to make a cloak. Her bare feet spread out before her and the hides over her knees, she is sweating a little—at the throat, along the line of her upper lip—and she stops occasionally to push the wet hair from her brow with the back of her hand. She catches me looking at her and meets my eyes with her own. She has stopped being scared of me, or puzzled, or even amused. I am just another member of her father-in-law's household, where she is a stranger like myself now that her husband is dead. She is listening to the old man, who is telling the boy a story as he works away at a net. I too listen. I am the only one here who is idle, and I let the strange words fill my head, understanding nothing, but fascinated nonetheless to hear the old man assume some other voice than his own, deeper, gruffer—the child's eyes open in wonder—or a high-pitched womanish voice that makes the child lift up his shoulders and giggle and draws from the old woman behind us one of her crowlike caws.

The old man's story is full of wonders. Is it, I ask myself, about a wolf? A bear? Some demon spirit? The young woman, who has heard all this before, watches the child in anticipation, laughing when he laughs and catching my eye so that I laugh too. When the old man's voice evokes—what?—a wizard, one of the gods?—her fingers stop working a moment and her eyes darken.

Somewhere deep in myself I know this story. I have heard it before. In childhood. From one of our slaves perhaps, though in another language. It is the tune that I recognize.

The old man's voice weaves through the air as it darkens around us. We are moving into winter, into night. His hands, which are square and roughened, work steadily at the net. He is a craftsman. I recognize that. One sees immediately the sureness of his touch. He is too deeply absorbed in his story, in his working of the net, to be aware of us, except when the child laughs or touches his knee a moment in fear.

I call him old, though we must be pretty much of an age, and I am not yet fifty. The harshness of his life, and the rigors of this place, have weathered and tanned and lined him so that he has the appearance, to a Roman eye, of a man of seventy. Blocky, tough as I have never been, with his shaven head and whiskers, he has an air of stern nobility.

I try to imagine his life, that must year after year have run parallel to my own, but no image appears. I cannot conceive of his childhood, or his youth, or picture the dead woman who was his wife, and whose grave outside the village I have seen him stop at once or twice on his way home from the harbor. His life, year after year, must have been just what I see now, work, sleep, work. And yet it seems mysterious to me, since what is not accounted for in it is his dignity, which makes me feel foolish and giddy. My life has been so frivolous. Brought up to believe in my own nerves, in restlessness, variety, change; educated entirely out of books, living always in a state of soft security, able to pamper myself, to drift about in a cloud of tender feelings, and with comfortable notions of my own intelligence, sociability, kindness, good breeding; moved by nothing that I couldn't give a name to, believing in nothing I couldn't see; never for a moment challenged by more than a clever boy can handle, who has learned early (too early perhaps) to turn all questions with elegance and a gloss of style—what can I know of the forces that have made this man, this tamer of horses, whose animal nature he somehow takes into himself and gentles? There is in his eyes, in his speech, in the powerful slowness with which he moves, something of the vast steppes from which they come, those horses, these tamers of horses, who when they die are not buried like other men but are left to ride above the earth in leagues of air.

Tomorrow I am to go with the old man's hunting party to the birchwoods, where there are deer.

When we assemble in the little yard it is frosty, and there are stars, hard, pointed, hanging low overhead.

We eat together at the bench: dishes of curd that have been thinned with water, warmed in a pot and sweetened with dark-tasting honey. The bees are wild, grazing on herbs deep in the brush, and the honey has some of the bitterness of those mysterious plants, and gives the curds a fragrance that fills the nostrils before its sweet aftertaste comes to the palate. The effect is not pleasant until you get used to it. But I am hungry and accept a second dish with the rest.

We are barely finished when the others arrive, wearing strapped leggings, shirts laced open across the chest, and carrying bows. There are three youngish men, looking fierce with their dark whiskers and long hair, and one old man, diminutive and gray, who is the village shaman. Behind them in a noisy rabble are half a dozen barefoot children.

My old man greets them, clasping hands with each in turn and embracing the shaman, who mutters words of blessing, not only to the old man but to each of the women, to the boy, to the benches, the doorposts, even to me.

We gather in a circle and fall silent. The boy goes off to where the pot stands warm in the yard, and his mother ladles into his hands a little of the curds we have eaten. The boy comes with it into the circle, and there is a stillness as the household demons assemble, creeping out from under the embers, from our empty bowls on the bench, from odd cracks and corners of the walls. The boy who is the center of all this looks nervous. His eyes move about the yard, from the fire to the bench, looking for the creatures whose interest for this moment is concentrated on him, on his cupped hands with their mixture of all the grains and weeds of the local fields, aware that he is, for the brief period of the ceremony, no longer himself—the youngest member of the household, a pudgy seven-year-old, more than usually spoiled and mischievous—but a conductor of dark forces, an embodiment of the house itself, breathing heavily in the silence, trembling, holding out to be tasted by invisible mouths the meager fruits of the earth.

The shaman begins to sing and is joined by the rest. The boy stiffens and shakes. When a little of the gruel

41

spills from his hands, and after a moment's doubt he lowers his head to lick at it, the old man, without ceasing his chant, clips the boy lightly over the ear. The gruel drips, and one of the young men, motioning to the boy that he is not to be blamed, draws the earth over it with his boot. The chanting ceases. We stand quiet. The boy's eyes shift anxiously and I see them move quickly to his mother, who nods, and then to his grandfather, who pats him lightly on the head. He turns stiffly, and we watch him, very carefully now, bearing his cupped hands before him, walk slowly back to the pot and spill the remains of the gruel on the fire. Which hisses. And with that, the circle breaks. Everyone laughs and begins talking at once, the yard is filled with activity as the men move away to resume their bows, the woman cleans the child's hands with a cloth, the two old men joke and slap one another's shoulders. All the signs, it seems, are propitious. We can go.

The horses—short, stocky beasts, with wooden saddles covered with cloth—are brought round now to the palisade entrance and we mount. The old man, who is a little ashamed for me in front of his neighbors, shows me how to ride without stirrups, by gripping the horse's flanks with my knees, and the younger men, out of politeness, busy themselves with their saddle straps. One of them whistles, looking away over the river flats to where the sun is just a wash of pale light on the eastern horizon, diffused and glowing in the mist. We ride down out of the village. The ground towards the marshes is white with frost, and our hooves as we pass leave big prints that immediately break up and spread, as if gigantic horsemen, like the ones in my dream, were walking invisibly behind us, placing their hooves very carefully in our tracks. Mist swirls in off the flats, round the breasts of our horses, round our knees. We might be wading through clouds. But high up there is yellow light, broken with ribs of cloud wrack, and the birds are singing.

Half an hour later, with the sun high over the brush-woods, a single red ball, the air is still cloudlike, thinning on the rises but as thick as surf when we dip down into the hollows.

We move slowly, the horses plashing through tussocky swamp, breathing heavily as we push uphill. All the land above the river flats is uneven, and we must keep to the uplands because the marshes are still flooded after the summer rains.

At last the mist begins to disperse. We have come out into a sparsely wooded landscape, all whitened stalks and spearlike grass heads, that is lighted gold and brown in the early sun. Rabbits tumble away from us in the brush, and the men laugh and halloo as the little white tails bob away. We are climbing now towards a wooded plateau beyond an outcrop of split rocks, that might, in another world, have been an old fortification. We push steeply up between the rearing granite walls, and at the head of the file I hear the first of the horses gallop away into what must be a clearing. Then as I come over the last of the grassy rise, with the horse very nearly slipping under me, I see.

It is a huge natural circle. The first of the horsemen has stopped about thirty yards off, and each of the others gallops up beside him. Then together, in line, they ride into a screen of pines blown ragged in the wind, with me just a little behind, since I realize that in coming up here we have made a detour; some ritual is being enacted in which I have no part. We move into the screen, over a carpet of soft needles, and the horses' hooves stir up their scent.

As the pinewood begins to thin, what lies beyond comes into view. At first I cannot guess what it is. Then I realize from the tales I have heard that it is a great circle of funerary mounds, a hundred of them perhaps, all made of broken stone and many of them still surmounted by the skeleton of a horse and rider, impaled on a pole, which is the proper burial for a horseman. I follow the riders around the great circle. Big birds go flapping away and climb in a circle above us. The wind shakes the poles, which clatter in their sockets, and I am reminded, by this ghostly army, of my dream. We ride around the circle, once, twice, a third time, then come to a halt. The headman takes from his shoulder a wallet full of grain, and suddenly leads the whole party off on a wild race amongst the dead, back and forth between the rattling poles and their skeletons, casting handfuls of grain to the dead mouths and shouting to scare away evil spirits and birds. I observe for the first time that there are stunted stalks of barley, wild oats, wheat even, all around me in the sunlight. We are in the middle of an immense field.

The men's yelling dies away and the old man rides up beside me, smiling, and offers me a handful of seed. I take it sheepishly, but fail at first to catch his intention. With a grin that shows all his bad teeth, he throws his head back and lets forth a bloodcurdling cry. Then nods and looks expectant.

Self-consciously, I repeat the sound. He smiles again, and still smiling, claps me on the shoulder. I ride off into the glittering circle, offering my feeble parody of a horseman's death cry and scattering my handful of grain.

Oddly enough as I weave back and forth between the towering forms I feel a moment of exhilaration, and am reminded of something—something that my mind just fails to grasp, as if all this had happened before. I shout again, louder, and make a narrow circuit of the field, as I have seen the others do, letting the cold air fill my lungs, then expelling it in a long cry, and feel freed of something. It is as if some fear went out on my breath and left my spirit clear. I am a Roman, I tell myself, trotting back to where the others sit, grinning broadly. I am a Roman and a poet. But that breath and the sound it carries still moves out from my body into the world, and I feel freer for it. The old man greets me with a handclasp. He says words that I do not understand, and as we ride off one of the young men holds his horse aside, so that I go down the steep defile immediately behind the headman, with the rest of the party behind.

Riding out into the sunlight I find myself thinking, for perhaps the first time in thirty years, of the brother who died when I was a young man, and whose place I took as my father's heir.

Thirty years ago. Riding just like this after his funeral, with my father at my side, I suddenly urge ahead and put a horse's length between us. He is angry with me, and I feel hurt, slighted, because I know what he is thinking: that of the two of us it is my brother who should have survived. I am the frivolous one, who will achieve nothing in the world. It is my brother who would have saved the last of our lands, won important public office, done all a good son can be expected to do in the way of piety towards his family gods. I know this is true and feel my life, my whole body's weight in the saddle, as a burden. I would do anything to be lying in the stone tomb, and to have him riding away in the sunlight with my father at his side. But pride has made me stubborn. And guilt. I have just told my father, as we move into single file, that I am leaving and will not return. I have already begun to leave—starting away from him on the narrow path from the grove and keeping the whole horse's length between us. I am already on my way to Rome. I am already, though I cannot know it yet, on my way to exile, setting out for this day, thirty years later, when I will be an old man riding with barbarians at the edge of the world, outside the Roman Law my father believed in so passionately, and the Roman State to which he dedicated our lives, with not a man now in nine days' riding distance who knows the Roman tongue. Who could have guessed, that morning, that we should ride so far from one another —that his curse upon me, unspoken perhaps, not even allowed to break the surface of his mind, should have carried me so far, and should have been, all these years, like a cold draught upon my back, even in sunlight.

Now, suddenly, the sunlight upon my back is warm. Somewhere, in all that barbaric shouting up there on the plateau, I had let them back into my life, the brother thirty years dead, the father buried only a year before my disgrace. It was for them that I was shouting. Rites that I had merely gone through the motions of at my father's funeral—a Roman son sacrificing, sprinkling a few cold drops for a Roman father—suddenly came alive in that shout and I was finished with the dead. Free, at last, to prepare a death of my own.

We enter the birchwoods of the hunting place towards midday.

The trees are already bare for the most part, their silvery trunks slashed with black, the last golden leaves caught in a broomstick of twigs, and the earth under our hooves sighing and sifting with the drifts of those that have already been shaken down. The sun is watery, the sky pale, the day windless. Almost unnaturally still.

One of the young men dismounts and leads his horse, stooping to examine the earth, where it is visible, for tracks. We all climb down and walk behind him, and he leads us to a wolf's den. The bitch stands at the entrance with her fangs bared, and her cubs, caught in the open, stop tumbling about on the earth, nipping at one another, little soft things, all fur, and as we come up start back and stand on all fours behind her, staring. We pass by, and later, find the tracks of a bear, and then deer tracks. And among them, astonishingly, though the others seem unsurprised, the prints of a human foot, bare, small, the prints perhaps of a child. The old man nods gravely and explains with signs. It *is* a child, a boy of ten or so, a wild boy, who lives with the deer. They found the prints first two seasons ago. And last year one of the hunters saw the boy but could not get close.

I am in a ferment. I have a thousand questions to ask them but can say nothing. Where does the boy come from? Who were his parents? How did he get here? How can he have survived, naked in all seasons, and with no one to feed or nurse him? Of course I have heard of such occurrences before. There are stories of wild children all over, but nobody, when you pin them down, has actually seen one. Then there are our Roman twins, the wolf brothers, the fathers of our state. Does anyone believe, I wonder, the actual facts of their legend—anyone, I mean, except a few simple peasants? But the child's prints are real. As real as the deer tracks beside them.

I touch one with my fingertips, and try to conceive, from that contact, the creature that has made the print. Beginning with some warmth I imagine I can feel, I conjure him up, I call him to mind. But this is absurd. The foot must have touched the ground for the merest flash of a second. The child was running, springing along over the leaves. You can tell by the depth of the impression, and how wide apart they are, these prints, that the child runs with the deer and can equal them in swiftness.

I touch one of them again. They seem miraculous. And suddenly, as if my imagination had indeed summoned him up, I see the child, and stranger still, recognize him. I, first of all of us, see him outlined against the blue light between two birches about fifty yards off, crouched like an animal, staring at us, a small boy as lean as a stick, with all the ribs of his torso showing under the tanned skin, bony elbows and knees, and straight black hair to the shoulders. He springs up at my cry and goes bounding away into the woods.

Did I really see him? Or did I see suddenly, after all these years, the Child who used to be my secret companion at Sulmo, and whose very existence I had forgotten. Suddenly he was there again before me. Was the vision real? I am skeptical. But the men believe. They mount quickly and go galloping off in the direction my arm is pointing, their hooves kicking up clods and showers of leaves; and at the same time half a dozen deer who have been grazing out of sight come skittering across the clearing towards me, swerving in panic as I shout and fall.

The men when they come back are full of a story they cannot get me to understand. Did they actually see the boy? Surely he cannot have outrun them. He must have gone to earth somewhere, in a wolf's lair, or deep into a trough of leaves, or under the roots of some tree. We ride slowly among the trees, weaving in and out among the silvery trunks, as in a dream, calling to one another to mark positions and keeping our eyes open for any sign of movement, our ears pricked for a sound. We startle odd groups of deer, and one of the young men shoots one and slings it across his shoulder to make our evening meal. All afternoon we circle round the same few hundred yards of forest as in a dream, till the evening mist begins to gather and the light fades. What will we do, I ask myself, if we see the boy? Give chase and capture him? Then what? And who is he? The day grows blue, shadows gather around us and the old man decides to make camp.

We tether the horses and the old man assigns each of us a task. Mine is to gather sticks for the fire. One of the young men also stays behind, to flay and butcher the deer, which he does swiftly and cleanly, hanging the whole skin over a branch and chopping the meat into haunches and chunks for roasting. The entrails he leaves to one side, together with a gourd filled with the first of the animal's blood.

I wander about, muttering to myself and making my pile of sticks, then sit hugging my knees and thinking of him: the Child.

Where is he? Is he still watching us from where he cannot be seen? What I remember clearly now are his eyes, fixed on me across the open space between the trees. That stare is something I could not have imagined. I have seen nothing like it before, except from the eyes of *my* Child, so many years ago. I have invented nothing like it in my poems, that were full of strange creatures caught between man and some higher or lower creature, in a moment of painful transformation. It exceeds my imagining, that sharp little face with its black stare, and I think how poorly my poetry, with its elegant fables and pretty, explainable miracles, compares with the accidental reality of this creature who must exist (if he does exist) not to impress but simply because he has somehow tumbled into being. I hug my knees and talk to myself in my own tongue, so that the young huntsman, who is covered with blood, but very open-faced and innocent looking, is alarmed and keeps away from me. When the others come back I see him speak to the old man, who glances shyly over his arm at me, and I have to shake myself back into society— if that is what it can be called, when I and these men have only the likeness of our humanity to share, and neither experience, custom nor tongue between us.

I watch the shaman spread out his symbols on the beaten grass. A fish-bone needle, a lump of river clay formed into a crude ball, a handful of seeds. He places these objects in a circle drawn around him with the bone, and I listen as he begins to rock back and forth on his haunches, drawing out of himself a high-pitched womanish voice like the one the old man uses in his tales, but higher far, more unearthly, as he lets it forth in little yelps and squeals or in long slow whistles, and sways above the earth. At last, when he falls still and seems asleep, his hands open before him, the young man who has killed and butchered the deer comes to the edge of the circle with his gourd of blood. He paints a little of it on the shaman's forehead with his fore-finger, touches the wrinkled lips, then pours a few drops into the shaman's hands. The rest he trails around the margin of the circle, and we sit outside, in the growing dark, till the shaman begins to speak, half a dozen syllables repeated over and over again in his own voice, with little yelping sounds of the other voice between. Then suddenly he wakes and it is over. He has, while we watched, been on a dream journey to the distant polar regions. His spirit has been there, moving fast over the frozen steppes across the river into the grinding wastes, and it is the voice of the polar spirits we have heard through him. Now suddenly he is one of us again, a perfectly ordinary old man, hungry, a little stiff in the joints, moving about on his buckled legs to help make a fire and to strap birch branches together in a high conical shelter.

Does the boy watch all this, I wonder? And what

does he make of it? What species does he think we might belong to? Does he recognize his own?

I think this all the time I am chewing the thick deer steaks and sucking my fingers clean, and afterwards while the men sing together—an eerie sound out there in the empty woods. Does he hear it? What creatures does he think might make such noises? Has he discovered that he too can draw sounds out of himself by means of his breath? Has he discovered the rudiments of speech? Does he speak to himself, having no other creature with whom to share his mind, his tongue? Being in that like myself.

I fall asleep thinking such thoughts, and half wake to find myself alone, with only the stars overhead, then fall into a deeper sleep, and dream; or wake again, I cannot tell which. I am conscious anyway that some animal has come up out of the dark and is staring at me. A wolf? Is it a wolf's snout I can feel, a wolf's breath? A deer's? Or is it the Child? As in that earlier dream I am face to face with something that is not myself or of my own imagining, something that belongs to another order of being, and which I come out of the depths of myself to meet as at the surface of a glass. Is it the child in me? Which child? Where does he come from? Who is he?

I wake, and there is no one. On the other side of the fire, one of the young men, wrapped in a skin, turns over in his sleep and mutters incomprehensibly a few strange, thick-tongued syllables—whether in his own language or in the no-language of sleepers I cannot tell. Someone must have covered me against the cold. I lie for a moment looking up at the stars, which seem very close, and they fade into me, through me. When I wake again it is dawn.

The winter has come and gone. We are already deep into spring. The days are watery blue and the wind blows mild, but there is no blossom to be seen. The scrub is grayish green rather than black, the sea throbs and burns. But there are no orchards to break into bud, no violets, no shade trees to show their pale green fronds, no streams to bubble and braid in the sunlight.

Winter has been terrible beyond belief. For seven months the wind from the pole comes howling in across a thousand miles of open grassland, flattening the brush, whipping the sea into black foam, till at last the whole ocean freezes, and you can walk out from the shore upon it and see the fish motionless below. The brackish pools from which the women draw our drinking water grow solid, and it is the men who go out now to chip lumps of it that they haul back to be melted, as we need it, over a flame. Impossible to venture out in that freezing gale without a flapped cap and wrappings of fur, a cloak, boots, leggings—and even then the breath freezes, the beard forms icicles that snap and tinkle. A man's speech might be chipped off in the same manner as our drinking water and melted later in the warmth of the house, if anyone dared open his mouth out there to pass even the time of day. We move about it in a dream, as if our wits had turned to sharp little crystals in our head. As if, like bears and other such creatures, we had crawled deep into some cave in ourselves and fallen asleep, moving about only as dream figures, stiff, unseeing, as we pass in and out of each other's lives.

My mind moves out continually to the deer forest and the Child. How does he survive out there? Naked. Unhoused. I see him often in my sleep, a ghost moving over the snow among the birches, chewing at lichen, digging under the ice for mold. Can he survive this season? Will the men find his tracks next year? I am impatient for the weather to soften so that I can urge the old man, Ryzak, to make up a party and search for him. It is my secret. I will speak out nearer the time. It is what keeps me alive in all this. Meanwhile, night after night, I hunt the Child in my sleep. I warm him with my breath. Or is it the breath of some animal that warms him, wolf or deer, even there in my dreams? Or does he perhaps sleep out the winter like one of the creatures, curled up in some hollow and tied to the continuance of things only by his own slow breathing? And if so, how is he fed? And what does he dream of? Does he dream?

He is the wild boy of my childhood. I know it now. Who has come back to me. He is The Child.

Two events give shape to these white months. One was the first news in our village, cried from street to street and beaten out with wooden gongs, that the Dacians had taken and burned one of the towns to the north and were streaming toward us over the river. The other, which followed almost immediately, was their attack on us.

The river, long before the year's end, had begun to

freeze. Five-thousand paces wide, it was now a bridge of solid ice, and the Dacian horsemen, hundreds of them, poured down from the northern plain and were thundering across it. We had to man the walls of our village against them, and I too was called upon to turn out with one of the companies, given a lance and helmet—I who have lived through fifty years in an empire at peace with itself and never done a day's drill—and sent to stand behind the palisade in the cold night air, unrecognizable under my mountain of fur.

I am taken with the irony of it. As a Roman citizen of the knightly order, the descendant of a whole line of warriors, with the law and the flower of Roman civilization to protect against the barbarians, I scoffed at such old-fashioned notions as duty, patriotism, the military virtues. And here I was, aged fifty, standing on guard at the very edge of the known world. To protect what? A hundred or so mud and wattle huts, three hundred savage strangers who do not even speak my tongue. And of course, my own skin.

As it happened, on the night the raiders came I was in bed, and had to be shaken awake by one of the women. I heard it too then. The thunder of their hooves on the ice, the wooden gongs beating, the voices in the dark. Ghostly figures out of the north, out of my dream, galloping in across the wide arc of moonlight that was water only a few weeks ago. I stumbled out. Arrows rained out of the sky and fell in the thatch, struck a poor fellow watching at the corner of the stockade, and he fell, writhing. The arrows are tipped with poison. The wound festers and stinks, and for three days the man whose body has been struck is in delirium, finding his way slowly out into the grasslands beyond the river to the place where the earth will receive him. All night they swirled round and round the stockade, yowling, yelping like wolves, and the arrows fell. In the morning they were gone, and all the brush to the southeast was aflame. Great clouds of smoke rolled back over us, black, bitter with the smell of thorns.

They have passed on to one of the settlements on the Thracian side. And now it is spring.

I have spoken to the old man about a search party (I have enough of their language now to make the most pressing of my wants known to people) but he seems unwilling to commit himself. Is he afraid? Does some superstition exist about the Child? Was the shaman's trance song, which I took to be some sort of blessing on the deer hunt, in reality a ceremony for the Child? Where do these people believe the Child comes from? The gods? Do they think he is one of their own people? Is he? Or a child perhaps from the grasslands to the north, who has been lost here in one of the raids?

I have not told the old man that I know the Child, and used to speak to him when I was a boy at Sulmo. Nor have I admitted to him that I want to capture the boy and bring him here among us. Only that I need to assure myself that he has survived into another season; which the old man believes readily enough, since they think me mad anyway, endlessly in a ferment about things they care nothing for, fussing about notions in my own head. But day after day the old man makes excuses. The palisade has to be repaired, and they have to make a long trip north to the pine forests for timber. Then an old man in the village dies, and the whole male population has to make a two-day funeral journey to see him interred. Then the fish are running. A whole week is taken up while the men row out with nets day after day and take them. Then another period when they go out with lanterns after the squid. Is the old man simply humoring me? Must we wait, as before, for autumn?

It is autumn. Tomorrow we go again to the birchwoods after deer. I dare not mention the Child. We ride out in the same way as before, make the same detour up to the plateau and through the screen of pines to where the dead ride high on their fleshless horses. Only this year the cold has come early. The plateau is in cloud, gray mists swirl across before us and the poles click and sway. The shouts of the men as they ride round scattering their handfuls of seed are dampened by fog, cut off and blown back into their throats.

On the way to the woods it drizzles. There are no tracks. The earth underfoot is soggy and the horses splash through puddles of brilliant blue light amongst the leaves, or through dirty-gray clouds. We hunt deer. Flay them, butcher the meat and load it in panniers. There is no sign of the Child. The other men look anxiously about them and are glad when we can get away. I am crazy with disappointment and grief. Another winter. How can he survive? How can I survive, without knowing he is still there?

Another spring.

I understand all that is said to me now in this crude tongue, by these plain but kindly people. I have begun to teach the old man's grandson Latin, to write it, and to recite poems. Some of them my own. He is a bright child, but of a sullen disposition, and he sees no use in what he learns. Listening to the old man now, telling his stories in our little yard, I know what the different voices signify: they are the north wind, they are wolves, they are giants, they are the ghosts of warriors, they are a shinbone, a severed head, they are the bottom of the sea. The old man's stories are fabulous beyond anything I have retold from the Greeks; but savage, a form of extravagant play that explains nothing, but speaks straight out of the nightmare landscape of this place and my dream journeys across it. Our civilized fables that account so elegantly for what we see and know seem feeble beside these elaborate and absurd jokes the old man mutters over. They are like winter here. They fill the world. They make the head buzz, they numb the blood. They seem absolutely true and yet they explain nothing. I begin to see briefly, in snatches, how this old man, my friend, might see the world. It is astonishing. Bare, cruel, terrible, comic. And yet daily he seems nobler and more gentle than any Roman I have known. Beside him I am an hysterical old woman. Utterly without dignity.

It begins to be autumn again. There is a smokiness in things. Once again we go to the birchwoods.

Almost immediately, in the golden light of a fine autumn day, with the sky broken in rainpools among the drifts of yellow leaves, he is there, standing quite still and taller after these two years, among the slashed birches. I am filled with joy. He is there. He is real. The others see him too. He is streaked with mud, with bony knees and elbows and a shrunken belly. An ugly boy of eleven or twelve with a bird's nest of dirty hair.

We are sitting, five of us, in a circle, drinking a little of the thin soup we have brought with us, while the horses wander among the birches, grazing off what blades of grass still push up through the leaf mold. It is late afternoon. Still. We hold our cups in both hands, drinking, not speaking, and suddenly the boy is there, watching us. The men's eyes dark over the rim of the cup and their fingers grimy. We all look. First at the boy then at one another, and are frozen. Even the horses cease grazing and raise their heads against the watery blue of the afternoon, sniffing, scenting another presence. I can hear our breathing. It is as if we were all, for a moment, charmed. As if time had stopped. And I feel that if we could sit like this long enough, cross-legged on the leaves, so that we seemed like another part of the wood; if we let our spirits out, shaking them loose, and became wood, leaf mold, lichen—he would come to us. The others, I know, are afraid. Their stillness is a sort of terror. These men who are not afraid of whirling horsemen in the night with poisoned arrows and firebrands, or of a wild boar with its tusks foaming, are afraid of the Child. I am not. My stillness is for fear that we may, even with the lifting of a finger or the catching of a breath, startle him into flight.

So we sit—for how long?—and stare at one another. He does not startle. But one of the horses, lowering its head to nibble, moves across between us, and when it passes, the space between the birches is empty of all but light.

I am calmer now. He is still there, that is what matters. There is time for the rest. We shall stay two nights in the birchwoods.

The first night, just at the edge of the fire's circle, where the dark begins, I set a bowl of gruel: mixed grain seed boiled in brackish water and flavored with honey. For hours after the others sleep I sit wrapped in my cloak, straining to hear a footfall among the leaves. I know he must come to watch. He has begun to look for us, I know that, as we look for him. He feels some yearning toward us, some need to satisfy himself about who we are, and why we have a shape, a smell, so unlike that of the other creatures of the forest. Has he begun to ask of what kind he is? Does he guess that some part of us, at least, is of his kind? As we know that in shape at least he is of ours.

I listen but hear nothing. I fall asleep, still sitting upright against a birch trunk, and am woken by the first silvery light of dawn. I scramble across to the bowl. It is empty. Something has come and lapped up the gruel. A deer? One of the forest demons these people worship? The Child? I hide the bowl under my cloak and pretend I have been to relieve myself but the old man watches me and knows. He thinks this is all folly. And dangerous folly. He is too much ashamed of me, and my old man's silliness, to let me see that he knows. He orders the young men about in a voice louder and gruffer than usual as if he were trying to frighten the Child away.

It is a clear still day and the deer are everywhere. The men hunt and kill five or six of them, and our camp in the clearing is like a butcher's shop, the smell of blood is all over us, the skins hang dripping from branches, joints of meat—haunches, legs, rib-halves—are stacked ready for packing. The women will salt and store them against the winter. The work takes us all day. We will spend a second night here and be off at dawn.

Again I set out the bowl of gruel, and this time sleep on the far side of the fire, propped up hard against a tree trunk and determined not to doze.

I fall asleep almost immediately, and dream. What I half thought in the woods yesterday, while we were watching the Child, is true. We have all been transformed, the whole group of us, and become part of the woods. We are mushrooms, we are stones—I recognize my companions. I am a pool of water. I feel myself warm in the sunlight, liquid, filled with the blue of the sky; but I am the merest broken fragment of it, and I feel, softly, the clouds passing through me, their reflections, and once the suddenness of wings. Slowly it grows dark. A breeze shivers my surface. And as darkness passes over me I begin to be afraid. My spirit hovers somewhere close and will, I know, come back to me when I wake. But I am afraid suddenly to be just a pool of rain in the forest, feeling the night creep over me, feeling myself grow cold and fill with starlight, feeling the temperature drop. I consider what it might be like to freeze. I imagine that. But only at the edges of myself, as the first ice crystals click into shape. It is fearful. What would happen to my spirit then? I lie in the dark of the forest waiting for the moon. And softly, nearby, there are footsteps. A deer. The animal's face leans toward me. I am filled with tenderness for it. Its tongue touches the surface of me, lapping a little. It takes part of me into itself, but I do not feel at all diminished. The sensation on the surface of me is extraordinary, I break in circles. Part of me enters the deer, which lifts its head slowly, and moves away over the leaves. I feel part of me moving away, and the rest falls still again, settles, goes clear. What if a wolf came, I suddenly ask myself? What if the next tongue that touched me were the wolf's tongue, rough, greedy, drinking me down to the last drop and leaving me dry? That too is possible. I imagine it, being drawn up into the wolf's belly. I prepare for it.

Another footfall, softer than the first. I know already, it is the Child. I see him standing taller than the deer against the stars. He kneels. He stoops towards me. He does not lap like the deer, but leaning close so that his breath shivers my surface, he scoops up a handful, starlight dripping from his fingers in bright flakes that tumble towards me, and drinks. I am broken again. The disturbance is fearful, a noisy crashing of waves against the edges of me. And when I settle he is gone. I am still, reflecting starlight. I sleep. I wake.

It is still dark. The Child, I see, is just setting the bowl down. He is stooped, holding it in both hands, his face covered by the hanks of coarse hair.

He hears me draw breath. He is no more than ten feet

away and our eyes meet for a moment, before he drops the bowl. It rolls towards me. He springs to his feet and stands there, puzzled, as if uncertain, for the first time perhaps, which of the two worlds he should fly to— back into the woods, or into whatever new world he has smelled and touched and taken into himself that comes from us. He has eaten from an earthenware bowl made by men, on a wheel. He has eaten grain that has been sown and gathered and crushed and boiled, and sweetened with a spoonful of honey. Something, as we face one another in the darkness, has passed between us. We have spoken. I know it. In a language beyond tongues.

Next year there will be no need to hunt him. He will seek us out.

Only now he backs slowly away into the darkness, his bare feet scuffing the leaves, and I must wait for another whole winter to pass.

It all happens as I knew it would.

The year has passed quickly. I have become sturdy and strong again and have stopped mooning about and regretting my fate. I go for long walks in the brush-wood, which is full of tiny animals and insects, all of them worth observing. I climb down to the shore and talk to the fishermen, while the sea grinds and rattles at the smooth black pebbles. The sea in these parts is full of strange fish, all beautiful in their way, all created perfectly after their own needs, every detail of their anatomy useful, necessary, and for that reason admirable, even when they are the product of terror. I have stopped finding fault with creation and have learned to accept it. We have some power in us that knows its own ends. It is that that drives us on to what we must finally become. We have only to conceive of the possibility and somehow the spirit works in us to make it →actual. This is the true meaning of transformation. This is the real metamorphosis. Our further selves are contained within us, as the leaves and blossoms are in the tree. We have only to find the spring and release it. Such changes are slow beyond imagination. They take generations. But it works, this process. We are already the product of generation after generation of wishing to be thus. And what you are reader, is what *we* have wished. Are you gods already? Have you found wings?

I go out each day with the old man. He is the closest friend I have ever had. How strange that I have had to leave my own people to find him. He has taught me to weave a net, and I begin to be good at it. There are different sorts of nets, and traps also, for the different kinds of fish. There are also the various hooks. I am happy to learn all this. What is beautiful is the way one thing is fitted perfectly to another, and our ingenuity is also beautiful in finding the necessary correspondence between things. It is a kind of poetry, all this business with nets and hooks, these old analogies.

I have also begun to gather seeds on my excursions in the brush—there are little marsh flowers out there, so small you hardly see them, and when I come back I push them into the earth with a grimy forefinger and they sprout. I have begun to make, simple as it is, a garden.

And all winter I drilled with my company of guards

and have discovered in myself what my father must always have known was there, however much I denied it, the lineaments of a soldier. How I have changed! What a very different self has begun to emerge in me!

I now understand these people's speech almost as well as my own, and find it oddly moving. It isn't at all like our Roman tongue, whose endings are designed to express difference, the smallest nuances of thought and feeling. This language is equally expressive, but what it presents is the raw life and unity of things. I believe I could make poems in it. Seeing the world through this other tongue I see it differently. It is a different world. Somehow it seems closer to the first principle of creation, closer to whatever force it is that makes things what they are and changes them into what they would be. I have even begun to find my eye delighted by the simple forms of this place, the narrower range of colors, the harsh lines of cliff and scrub, the clear, watery light. Now that spring is no longer to be recognized in blossoms or in new leaves on the trees, I must look for it in myself. I feel the ice of myself cracking. I feel myself loosen and flow again, reflecting the world. That is what spring means.

I have also, in a winter of long evening arguments, won my battle with Ryzak. In the autumn, when the birches are bare, we will go out and find the boy, and this time, if it can be managed without harm, we will bring him back. Ryzak has only one doubt. He must first get the assurance of the shaman that they can bring the boy into the village without antagonizing some spirit of the woods.

What they are afraid of, I think, is that by allowing

the Child into the village they may make themselves vulnerable to whatever being it is that has raised and protected him. It may be the wolves that prowl round the stockade in winter, howling above the wind, gray packs that are themselves like spirits of the winter plains, shaggy, iron-fanged, famished with cold. Might the boy, Ryzak wonders, have the power to turn himself into a wolf in the winter months? Is that how he survives? And where would we be then? Might he be able to creep out at night and open the gates to his brothers? Or is it some spirit even more savage and terrible than wolves that has nursed him? Some animal presence we do not know and have never seen. What if he were in communion with that, or had the power of assuming the form of a creature whose shape, whose horror, we can only imagine, and have no magic to placate?

I argue that he is just a boy, a male child as human as ourselves, and Ryzak believes me, or pretends to, because he has a great desire, in my presence, to appear superior to his superstitious people and as reasonable as he thinks I am.

But in fact I am deceiving him. I know it is not an ordinary boy. It is the Child.

The summer comes, and my garden flourishes. Wild flowers mostly that I have found in the marshes or between the stalks of oats in our narrow ploughed land. Who knows where the seeds blow in from? Careful tending has made them strong, and regular feeding with leaf mold and manure brings out their color, blue, red, yellow. The women of the house find so much effort spent on something that we cannot eat foolish beyond belief; but they like the colors and are happy enough to provide me each day with a little water from our meager store. Mostly, I think, they humor me as they would a child. Everything else about us exists purely for use. The women wear no ornaments. What they sew has good strong seams but not a stitch that is fanciful. Only my flowers are frivolous, part of the old life I have not quite abandoned. Only the time I spend upon them is play.

For these people it is a new concept, play. How can I make them understand that till I came here it was the only thing I knew? Everything I ever valued before this was valuable only because it was useless, because time spent upon it was not demanded but freely given, because to play is to be free. Free is not a word that exists, I think, in their language. Nothing here is free of its own nature, its own law.

But we are free after all. We are bound not by the laws of our nature but by the ways we can imagine ourselves breaking out of those laws without doing violence to our essential being. We are free to transcend ourselves. If we have the imagination for it.

My little flowerpots are as subversive here as my poems were in Rome. They are the beginning, the first of the changes. Some day, I know, I shall find one of our women stopping as she crosses the yard with a bag of seed to smell one of my gaudy little blooms. She will, without knowing it, be taking the first step into a new world.

Meanwhile I think only of the Child. The rest is mere

filling of empty time. The summer passes with flowers. The grain is brought in, threshed, stored. It is autumn again.

We go out to take him.

I have no wish to tell how it came about. Coward that I am, I did not take part in the chase and would have preferred not to witness it. Crouched against one of the birches with my hands over my ears, I let the others do it for me, the big horses surging about the wood, chopping at the leaf mold with their iron hooves, the men whooping and yelling, weaving in circles, so that the Child, driven this way and that in the thick undergrowth, must have been confounded utterly by strange cries coming at him from all directions, shadowy figures darting out from all parts of the sky. When he suddenly stumbled into the clearing and stopped before me, he was in a state of utter panic, exhausted, half-crazed, his shoulders torn and bleeding where twigs had caught them, his body filthy with mud. His mouth, as he stood there surrounded at last, poured out a terrible howling that was like nothing I have ever heard from a human throat.

But as the first of the young men swung down behind him, he suddenly discovered a new force of energy, lashing out with fists, heels, teeth, till the young man covered his mouth and nostrils with a fierce hand, squeezing the breath out of him, and the others were able to hold and then tie him with thongs. Only the eyes continued to move wildly, and I thought from the spasms that shook his body that he might be in a fit.

I put my hand on him, and a savage hissing came from the nostrils, the spasms increased. At last we left him to himself, trussed like a pig, under an oak tree, while the shaman began his ritual. The high singing of the shaman's other, polar, voice seemed to quiet him. It was as if the shaman were singing the wildness from him, leading it north in his trance towards the polar circle of eternal whiteness, taking it down through a hole made with a fish bone, under the ice. When the shaman woke and came out of his circle the Child was asleep, and he slept like that all through the journey back, slung forward over the headman's saddle, and for another whole day after we had returned.

What a strange procession we must have made, coming up the long slope from the marshes in the late afternoon, with the autumn light over the river flats and the long black line of the cliffs, beyond which, shining flat and gray, lay the sea. Children left off splashing about in the pools and ran shouting behind us, wide-eyed, staring. Women gathering their clothes off thornbushes came and stood with their arms full of washing to watch us, only their eyes visible under the black shawls. Rumor of the boy's capture had preceded us. The lean body, about the size of a deer, slung across the headman's horse, might have been lifeless, drained of blood and spirit like the joints we were bringing home on the other horses.

But the news is already abroad that the creature, whatever he is—wolf boy, godling, satyr—is alive. The village has accepted him within its walls. It is all to begin.

III

WHAT have I done?

The Child is lying, still trussed, in a corner of the room opposite me. Since the first occasion the women have refused to touch him. When he fouls himself I must wash him down. They prepare his food, a gruel made of meal and sweetened with honey, but will not cross the threshold of the room. I untie his hands and leave the bowl, listening at the door for him to drag himself over the rushes and sup it up, snuffling like an animal in his hunger. He whimpers but does not cry. His eyes remain dry and nothing like a human sobbing ever comes from him, none of that giving of oneself over to tears that might release the child in him. The whimpering comes from somewhere high in his head and has been learned from one of the animals. He keeps it up for hours on end. To comfort himself, quite shamelessly, as some children suck their thumb, he excites himself with his hand to a series of little shudders, as I have seen monkeys do, then again, and again, till the spasms have exhausted him and he is quiet, squatting in the corner with his knees drawn up sharp and his mouth clenched; or curled up in a ball in the rushes, his knees under his chin, his elbows tight between them.

We spend hours simply staring at one another. And I have no idea what feelings might be at work in him. He shows no sign of interest in anything I do. I write a little. I eat. I mend a tear in my cloak. He stares but does not see. At first when I touched him in the cleaning he tried to bite me with his sharp incisors. Now he accepts all that I do with a passivity that has begun to disturb me. I am afraid we may already have killed something in him. I have a terrible fear that he may die —that what we have brought back here is some animal part of him that can be housed and fed for a while, and kept with us by force, but only till it realizes that the spirit is already gone, having slipped away out of the arms of that first young man who caught and held him; or worse still, having been dreamed out of his body in that first protracted sleep.

I watch him sleep. His limbs twitch like a dog's, with little involuntary spasms along the inside of the thighs.

Does he dream? If only I could be certain he was dreaming I would know that what I have to contact at last, what I have slowly to lead up through the ladders of being in him, is still there. I must know that he can dream. I must assure myself that he can smile, that he can weep.

But I have not even described him.

He is about eleven years old, tall, strongly but scraggily made, with the elbow and knee joints enlarged and roughly calloused. There are sores on his arms and legs and old scars that appear as discolorations of the flesh, brownish under the yellow tan. The limbs are lightly haired, the chest hairless; but all along the spine there is a hairline, reddish in color like a fox, and it is this that terrifies the women and has made them unwilling to touch him, though the phenomenon is common enough. You may observe it in small children everywhere, as they play naked on doorsteps or splash about in summer under water showers. It usually goes unremarked. Only in this boy has it become, for the women, some sort of sign. That and the feet, which are splayed and hardened from being unshod in all weathers, the toenails worn away, the underside of the foot thickened to a crust as deep perhaps as an earthenware dish, but in no way resembling anything other than a normal foot. The rumor that he is covered with hair and has hooves, which the boy Lullo brings back from the village, is absurd.

I dragged the boy in this evening and made him look at the Child and tell me what he saw. But he was too terrified to look properly, and though he has seen what there is to see, I know he is not convinced. What he imagines is so much more powerful than the facts.

I know what he thinks. He thinks I have somehow bewitched the Child's hooves into stunted feet to deceive him, or that I have bewitched *him*.

I had imagined that the boy, being something like the same age as the Child, might have some special interest in him, some special sympathy. But he has none. He regards the Child with loathing, as if he were somehow about to be displaced here by a changeling; as if—is it that?—the Child might, while he was sleeping, steal his spirit. These people believe profoundly in sleepwalkers and stealers of souls. Do they suspect, as I have begun to do, that the Child has lost his spirit, and may, while we see him curled asleep in his corner, be capable, like the shaman, of walking out of his body, through the walls into the next room, and into the boy Lullo's body while he is absent on one of those dream journeys small boys are accustomed to make, into the hunting woods or out over the river? The old woman and the boy's mother, I know, are encouraging him in this, because of his influence with the old man. But Ryzak, for what reason I do not know, remains my supporter in the business. Against the women. And against the shaman, who has come only once to examine the Child, and on that occasion refused to sing—another fact that the women mutter over and hold against me. The shaman and the women, of course, are in league.

So all day we sit in the half-dark.

I have come to guess a little of what the Child thinks by examining his features, but at no time have we communicated as before, when we spoke to one another in the woods. It is as if the spirit in him that I spoke to then were no longer present. I watch the mouth with its small, broken teeth. He has a way of drawing his lips back over them and taking the breath in sharp as if he were in pain; though he makes the same gesture, I notice, when he is exciting himself, and it is in this gesture that the odd bone structure is revealed, the high cheekbones, the pointed chin, the lines of the jaw. The eyes too I watch. They are very black, and deep set. The eyebrows tilt upward. The hair, which we have washed and cropped a little, is inky black, straight, and coarse in texture, not at all silky or fine; though this may be because he is undernourished or because his spirit is so low in him, or no longer there at all. I have noticed before how the hair takes on the shine or the dullness of the spirit, especially in the ill. He still seems, for all our scrubbing, less than clean. As if the earth had got so deep into his skin that he has taken on its color. It is perhaps dirt in the old wounds that accounts for the brownish scars on his limbs. He is not at all beautiful, as I had imagined the Child must be. But I am filled with a tenderness, an immense pity for him, a need to free him into some clearer body, that is like a pain in my own.

I think and think. What must the steps be? How should I begin? Kindness, I know, is the way—and time. To reveal to him first what our kindness is, what our kind is; and then to convince him that we belong to the same kind. It is out of this that he must discover what he is.

But we have begun so badly. How can he possibly think of us as anything but cruel? Which of the beasts would have done this to him? Which of the beasts would hunt him down on horseback, truss him up, carry him away from all he has ever known? Then there is the spitefulness of the boy, who I have decided must be kept away. And the hostility of the women.

In the end I must do it all myself. I must, at first, be the only one he has contact with.

I think, strangely, of the wolf in my dream that threatened to consume the whole pool of my being, and begin to be afraid.

The weeks pass.

I no longer leave the room now when the women bring his food. At first he was wary, as if perhaps I had set a trap for him as before. He edged towards the bowl, sniffed, examined it, took it in his hands, and all the while as he ate, more slowly than before, watched me over the rim with his deep black eyes, which seemed these times to have points of red. Then when he had cleaned out the last of the stuff with his finger, he rolled the bowl over the floor and dragged himself back to his corner, where he crouched with his knees up, waiting for me perhaps to make some move. Now he eats without being aware of me. As if I were not there. Grunting as he feeds.

I have also brought my straw pallet into the room, and sleep in the corner opposite him. He has got used to that as well. And I begin to feel again that I have been in contact with him, though it is impossible to know when the contact occurred. It may have been while I was washing him. He submits to that easily enough, though with no sense of his being touched in any part of his real body. It may have been in some chance meeting of the eyes as we pass in and out of each other's sight. Or it may have been in our sleep, as we move through this room in the same liquid medium, as if floating together in a pool, some casual meeting of one dream with another, a flowing into his sleep, or of his sleep into mine, at some point that the waking mind would not know of. Or in stirring about here, one part of the invisible current I make as I write, as my pen dips in the ink and my hand moves across the parchment, or as I drag the razor over my chin, may have broken against him so that he felt it. Who can tell? But I am certain now that the contact has been made. He no longer whimpers, or rocks back and forth on his knees, making little growls at the back of his throat. He watches. And I begin to believe that something I will have to call his mind has been engaged, and has started to move out into the room. I feel it. It is there after all. It is there. Some process of reaching up out of himself has begun of its own accord.

Today, while I was washing him, he laid his fingertips, with a kind of timid curiosity, on the back of my hand, feeling the texture of the skin—then drew back quickly, as if I might object and punish him. The effect was odd and a little frightening. As if an animal had come up in the dark and touched me with its tongue. Is he beginning to feel at last for some notion of his own being? Is it, for him, like touching his reflection in a glass? Has he, I wonder, any conception of what his own body is, what it looks like, what dimensions it possesses, how it displaces its own small part of the universe? Is it his body he must imagine first, and only after that come to a knowledge of what he is?

There is an intelligence. I feel it. More and more often now, as I settle into some work of my own, writing for example, I am aware of a separate center of energy in the room that disturbs my thoughts, that sets up eddies that beat like waves of light towards me and break against the edge of my consciousness. The room, I know, is filled with emotions that are not mine only, thoughts, not mine, that leap into the still damp atmosphere of a late morning where I sit scribbling and the boy, taut as a spring, watches out of his corner—the beginnings of a restlessness of mind, of body, that is the stirring in him of renewed life.

He is, after all, a child. He needs activity. His body needs to express itself in movement and his mind to reach out and touch and test things.

He has been here now for nearly two weeks. After those first three days when he slept, when his soul tried to bury itself in the earth, and these last days when he has lived in a state of half-sleep, he has begun to move again into wakefulness, into the full alertness of his youth. Yesterday, while I was out of the room briefly, he must have touched my writing materials. The ink was spilled. I sopped it up without giving any indication that I knew he had been tampering with things; refilled the pot; found my place in the roll. And almost burst out laughing to see that his tongue was blue.

Being out of the room again today, I stood just beyond the door frame and watched.

He shuffles across the floor towards the parchment roll and stares at it, pokes at it with his forefinger, then lowers his head and sniffs. How it must puzzle him that the roll still smells of animal hide. Once again the ink fascinates him. He sniffs at that also, but is careful not to spill it. He takes the stylus in his hand, and has been observant enough to grasp it clumsily, but correctly, between thumb and forefinger. He looks pleased with himself. He dips it in the ink, finding great difficulty in getting the pen, balanced as it is between his fingers, into the hole. He crouches over the pot, and there is on his face that look of utterly human concentration that one sees on the faces of small children when they are trying for the first time to draw, or make strokes for writing or thread a needle—the eyes fixed, the tongue pointed at the corner of the mouth and moving with each gesture of the hand, as if it too were one of the limbs we have to use as men, one of our means of pushing out into the world, of moving and changing its objects. Is that perhaps where speech begins? In that need of the tongue to be active in the world, like a hand among objects, grasping, pushing, shaping, remaking?

Watching behind the door these first attempts of the Child to handle the objects of his new world, I find my eyes wet with tears. There is something in our humanity, in the slow initiation of the creatures of our kind into all that we have discovered and made—in ourselves and in the world around us—that is always touching like this; one feels it in the first efforts of the child to push itself upright, to push that one step up that it must have taken our ancestors centuries to imagine and dream of and find limbs for; or in the first precarious placing of one block upon another to make a little tower, the beginnings of a city. All those ages of slow discovery. Relived by the child in just a few months, as he makes use of experience he can never himself have had, and which must lie latent in him, in the lives under his own of thousands long dead, whose consciousness he has somehow brought with him into the world. How much more moving then to see my Child make the discoveries that will lead him, after so many years of exile, into his inheritance, into the society of his own kind.

I have for several days now left his hands free. At

last, this morning, I untie all his bonds. They are no longer necessary. All that will tie him to us, to a new life, is invisibly there, he must feel it: the web of feeling that is this room, the strings—curiosity, a need to find out the usefulness to him of all these objects that surround him, and the way they define him and illuminate the uses of his own body—these are the threads that hold him now, and along which his mind must travel to discover how he is connected to us, to the bowl, the water scoop and bucket, the sponge I use to wash him, and which he has already begun to use himself, the ink pot, stylus and parchment, the colored ball I have placed casually where his eye cannot miss it, and which, since I never touch it, he must already have realized is his. I feel his mind moving out towards these things. I feel, even in darkness, the invisible twitching of strings.

For some reason, in these long hours of sitting with the Child, watching him move slowly out of himself, trying to imagine myself into his skin so that I will discover how it is I must lead him into his lost childhood, I have found myself more and more often slipping back into my own childhood—also lost until now, or rejected; certainly long forgotten. I fall into some timeless place in myself where the past suddenly reoccurs in all its fullness, or is still in progress. I am there again. I make contact with a self so surprising that I can scarcely believe it is me. I touch again on an experience that I recognize as mine only because its vividness can only be that of life lived in recall. Imagination could not present to the mind, to the senses, anything so poignantly real.

Of course all men put their childhood behind them. It is part of discovering a new self in manhood. But I have done so more than other men, I think. The simplicity of those early years at Sulmo fitted so ill with my new role as man about town, as sophisticated poet of the metropolis, that I should have felt only anxiety and some sense of disgust if I had tried to reconcile the two. For the same reason I found it painful to see my father, who remained disappointed in me—even after my literary reputation might have been enough to make up to him a little for my failure to become a man of affairs. He married again and had another family. And that too made it easy for me to keep away. I lived, after the end of my second marriage, as if I had sprung into the world complete with my first book of poems, an entirely new type, the creature of my own impudent views and with no family behind me, no tribe, no country, no past of any kind.

And now it all comes back to me.

Especially, and with feelings of an extraordinary tenderness such as I have not known for so long now that I cannot recall the last time they can have swept over me, certain evenings from my earliest childhood when we were turned over, my brother and I, to the women of the household, the farm servants, to be washed and dressed for bed, along with their own children, boys and girls both, who are of an age with us and are still at this time (since we have not yet learned to distinguish them as slaves) our playfellows in the farmyard and in the olive groves and orchards beyond.

In the big stone-flagged kitchen under the beams there are tubs of warm water and suds, and we children, perhaps a dozen or more, are splashing about together or paddling in pools on the floor, all shrieking and starting away wherever one of the women, their arms already holding the big fluffy white towels, reaches out and makes a grab for us. It is, to me, a scene of golden beauty and cleanliness. I feel my whole spirit washed at the thought of it: the clean naked bodies, the white towels, the women laughing and holding out their bare wet arms.

In these harvest days we are allowed to sleep out in the farmhouse with our nurse. My mother, who is sickly, and whose head aches with hay fever, has retired to her room and never appears. My father goes out each morning with the harvesters, and if the work is far off on the other side of the valley, he will stay out with the laborers overnight. We are put to bed with the others, on huge straw mattresses behind the kitchen, and lie awake while the women tell us stories about wood spirits and demons older than our Roman gods, who live in odd corners of the house and barn and must be placated with lumps of dough (which they come for in the guise of a mouse) or with herbs that only the oldest and wisest of the women know how to gather, high up in the hills.

This is a woman's world, which I will never know again. It smells of soapsuds and dough, of curds, of the raw wool I watch the older women carding on a terrace wall in the sun, with the fields behind them a glitter of wings. Early in the morning, almost before it is light, we go out together in a party, women and children, to

the water meadows, to gather big orange-yellow mushrooms. I watch the women, who are barefoot, haul their
skirts up in the dew while they squat to piss, their
heads upright under the straw panniers, and later, on
our way home, look on scandalized when, in the stubbled field, they stop and make mocking obeisance to
the scarlet-stained figures of Priapus that are set in the
midst of the wheat to scare off birds. Back in the yard,
there are eggs to gather from under the hens in their
wooden houses. There are pigs to feed. There is grain
to be winnowed by shaking it in the air in a basketwork
sieve. In the coolness of the kitchen, late in the afternoon, there are millet cakes to bake and to prick afterwards with a straw so that they will soak up honey.
And then, after dark, the bathing.

I watch again as one of the girls, her skirt hitched up
over her bare legs, her arms gleaming wet, takes my
brother by the prick and leads him round the tub like
a goose, while all the women throw their heads back
and laugh, and the children splash and clap their hands
and toss suds in the air. And I realize suddenly, nearly
fifty years after the event, that this must be the girl my
father is sleeping with. I see her lead my brother, the
little heir to all this world, round the sopping kitchen
floor while the women show their gapped teeth and
hold their sides and laugh. It is a vision of utter joyful-
ness; and I am at the center of it, understanding, for the
last time perhaps, a little of its mystery.

It is another world. How strange to find myself back
there for odd moments, knowing that I have made
nothing of whatever it was that was being revealed to
me then—that I went some other way, into a man's

world, into the city, into the state, as my brother too went another way, to death.

But stranger still is that all this time it has remained there, untouched, unrecalled, but still brightly new—and so real that I smell the raw cleanness of it still.

I think also, in these quiet hours, of my brother's death during the Parilia, just after our birthdays, which fall on the same day.

We have always been close, though our temperaments are so different; he is serious-minded, and filled with a deep sense of loyalty to things, to my father, to the farm, whose every boundary stone he knows, to the family, which is so closely bound up with the country here, the old tribal lands of the Peligni. He is deeply pious, in a way I respect and envy, but having taken on early my role as the frivolous one, I do as I am expected to do, and tease him about it.

For days he lies ill and cannot speak. He is just eighteen. I sit with him in a room off the courtyard, where he lies sweating on a daybed, breaking out in cold shivers, then burning. I read to him a little, but he cannot attend. I hold water to his lips and feel my hand trembling as he drinks. I weep and am ashamed of it. When the day of the Parilia comes I go out heavy-hearted as the twilight gathers to do the duty that is his, to do it for him, as he would do it, and am aware as I cross the yard of the women's eyes on me, and as I stride out across the fields to where the little fires are already blowing in the dark, I know that if I allow myself even for a moment to believe in the ceremony

I am about to perform, as he does, I will have replaced him, made him superfluous, since I will be assuring the gods (who do not exist) that I am there to take his place.

I wade uphill through the yellow grass, hardening my heart, though this in fact is a festival I have always loved, ever since I first went out on my father's shoulder to watch the fires lit and to see the men's shadows leaping amongst the corn.

I too know all the boundary stones of our land, but to me they mean something different. They are where the world begins. Beyond them lies Rome and all the known world that we Romans have power over. Out there, beyond the boundary stones, the mystery begins. My mind ventures out, touches the old worn boulders for luck, and then goes on in the dark, populating the unknown with what must be imagined since it cannot be seen. For my brother, I know, the farm and his mind are one. The stones glow at the edge of what he is: these fields that have been cleared of their pebbles and terraced, these ancient olives, with their gnarled trunks so thick that you can hide in them, as the wood spirits do, these vineyards, beehives, slopes of corn streaming with light under the moon. I walk through all this, feeling the grass heads brush my bare legs, and arrive at the field where my father is waiting.

He has already made his course and is drying his body with a cloth. I kiss him. I let a slave loosen my cloak. I sip from the pail of milk. Take in my hand the beanstalk and the ashes of the calf. My father dips a laurel branch in water and sprinkles me with it. He is weeping. My chest, my brow. I blink under the shower of little drops.

The heaps of straw are kindled all the way down the field for me to leap over, and as I sprint away and go flying over the first of them, feeling the rush of air into my lungs, feeling the joy of it, the leaping, the being cleansed and gathered into the web of things, smoke from the straws, dusky twilight, nightjars swooping after insects among the pines, the springing of the young plants under me, I know that it has happened— I have let some grain of belief in all this sprout in my mind, and killed him. My brother is dead. I feel it as a fact in my limbs, in their weariness as I come round to the start, in my own breathlessness as I lean forward, hands on hips, and gasp for air. I feel it, guiltily, in the glow that comes to my body after the exercise. I have run my brother's death. When they sprinkle me a second time with the laurel and I start back across the darkening fields, feeling my sweat dry in the breeze, it is to what I know has already occurred. I stop at the entrance to the yard and listen for the first wailings from the house, and hear them, the women's voices. Sitting at the edge of the field, in the dark, I loosen my sandals. I strew my shoulders, my legs, my hair, with earth and know obscurely what it is I am about. I am trying to wipe out the purification that was his, I am atoning for my own moment of belief.

So these things happen, deep in our lives. We do not speak of them. We hide them even from ourselves, but they do not leave us. For all our mockery of the earth we have come from, it covers us, we creep back to it, to its thickness on our limbs, its grit in our mouths. I killed something in myself on that night and tried to cover it with earth. Now it cries out in me again. I find myself wishing that I could talk to my father once more, after all these years of estrangement, and tell him that I have found my way back to that country I will never see again and am at home. I have admitted at last its claims upon me. I know where I was born.

And that brings my mind back, as always, to the Child. What is his country? What is his parentage? At what moment did he push out into the world, under what star sign, with what planet in the ascendant, in what ephemeris of the moon? And if he does not know ← these things can he ever know who he is or what his fate is to be?

Or does not knowing make him free?

Each morning now we go out, the Child and I, to practice our lessons in the open, where the boy and the women of the house cannot listen.

The Child carries the colored ball, which has become his talisman, his first possession among us; he never lets it go. In sleep he curls up around it. While eating he places it in the crook of his knee as he squats cross-legged with the bowl in his lap, handling awkwardly, at last, the wooden spoon I have taught him to use. When we are out walking he carries the ball in his left hand.

I avoid the places where we are likely to come across people from the village: women beating their clothes on the pebbles or laying them out to dry in the thorn-brush; men driving their ox ploughs to the narrow fields at the edge of the stockade where our meager crop of oats is grown. I avoid too the little grove to the west which is sacred to the women, and where at certain phases of the moon they sacrifice to Hecate with the entrails of a dog.

This leaves only the swampy land towards the river.

I take off my sandals (the boy goes barefoot, and bare except for a loose robe, which he tears off as soon as we are out of sight of the village) and we wade through the rushes to a turfy island covered with scrub and a few stalks of wild oats; and there, each morning, with the swamp birds invisible around us, creaking and calling, or climbing heavily into the watery sky, and the frogs tinkling, we begin.

I am teaching the Child to speak.

It is a difficult process. I have long since discovered on our expeditions together that he can imitate any of the birds or animals we come across, and he delights in showing off to me how he can whistle like the big hawks we see occasionally floating high up under the clouds or throw his voice, *pic pic,* against the bole of a tree, like the woodpeckers of my childhood, the sacred spirits of our Sulmo countryside. He stands with his feet apart, hands on hips, head held back to the light, and his lips contort, his features strain to become those of the bird he is mimicking, to become beak, crest, wattles, as out of his body he produces the absolute voice of the creature, and surely, in entering into the mysterious life of its language, becomes, for a moment, the creature itself, so that to my eyes he seems miraculously transformed.

Sometimes he uses his hands like an instrument to trill and flute, blowing across his fist and fluttering his fingers. At other times the cry simply floats out of him, high and clear, or the warbling comes from deep in his throat, a guttural murmuring, or his body suddenly gives forth a metallic creaking so that I am startled by its closeness. It is as if each of the various bird species —ground pigeons, crows, waders, high-flying migratory birds that have been who knows where over the horizon—had their life in him and could be drawn out on the breath between his lips; as if he had some entrance to their mysterious comings and goings among the grasses, or had been with them to the bottom of the river where the water birds dive after their prey, or in the high places of the air where imagination fails to follow them or to catch with the ear how their cries are translated at the margin of the stars.

Observing how he makes these sounds, and the sound of frogs, cicadas, rabbits, the low growl of wolves and their fearful baying, I get some clue at last to how he may be taught to speak.

His whole face is contorted differently as he assumes each creature's voice. If he were to speak always as frog or hawk or wolf, the muscles of his throat and jaw might grow to fit the sound, so intimately are the creatures and the sounds they make connected, so deeply are they one. It is through the structure of his own organs of speech then that he must learn to communicate. If I can reveal to him their physical shape he will discover their use.

For this reason, as I make the sounds I want him to imitate, and which he finds such difficulty in drawing up to his lips, I place his fingers on my throat so that he can hear the buzzing of my voice there, I lay his fingertips to my lips so that he can feel the shape of them, the flow of breath. Gradually, one sound at a time, we are finding human speech in him. It is a game he delights in. He is childishly eager to show me that he can imitate me as well as the creatures. With his fingertips at my lips, his brow furrowed, listening, he discovers the shape of his own lips, and the sound is almost perfect. He takes his hands from my throat and places them on his own, and laughs outright when he feels at last the same buzzing there and hears the sound; astonished at first, as if he didn't know where it came from, then jubilant, making the same sound over and over again in his triumph, with little whoops between.

I have begun to understand him. In imitating the birds, he is not, like our mimics, copying something that is outside him and revealing the accuracy of his ear or the virtuosity of his speech organs. He is being the bird. He is allowing it to speak out of him. So that in learning the sounds made by men he is making himself a man. Speech is the essential. I have hit at the very beginning on the one thing that will reveal to him of what kind he is. In making those buzzing sounds he discovers his throat. In intoning through his nostrils he realizes that he has a nose, and behind it, caverns where the sound reverberates. And so on for lips, tongue, teeth. As he builds up the whole range of sounds that we make, he is building up in his own head the image of head, checking and rechecking with his fingertips against my throat, my jaws, my lips, that he is made as I am, that he is man.

But what head is it that his imagination is creating?

What is it, finally, that I can lead him to imagine and then to become?

And having built up the whole repertory of sounds, what language am I to teach him?

Meanwhile we proceed with simple manual skills. I teach him to throw and catch the ball. He is quick at this and at all body skills and soon begins to play tricks on me, perceiving that I am neither as quick of eye nor as sure of hand and foot as he is. I teach him to cast a javelin, to thread and use a needle. He himself tries to hold a stylus and make marks with it. Strangest of all, he has learned to smile. Not simply to laugh in response to some clumsiness of mine as I dart about after the ball, but to smile, as we do, out of some state of his own soul, a sudden lighting up of the spirit in him that has no object and no cause. He also assumes, on our walks, the role of teacher, pointing out to me tracks in the grass and explaining with signs or gestures of his body, or with imitation sounds, which bird or beast it is that has made them. Or finding under the mold of a log a grub or chrysalis, he explains with his hands how it will be a moth, acting out in a kind of dance its transformation.

All this world is alive for him. It is his sphere of knowledge, a kind of library of forms that he has observed and committed to memory, another language whose hieroglyphs he can interpret and read. It is his consciousness that he leads me through on our walks. It flickers all around us: it is water swamps, grass clumps, logs, branches; it is crowded with a thousand changing forms that shrill and sing and rattle and buzz, and must be, in his mind, like the poems I have long since committed to memory, along with the names of a thousand gods and their fables, the rules of rhetoric, theorems, the facts of science, the facts of history, the theories of the philosophers. Only for him it is a visible world he can walk through, that has its weathers and its seasons, its cycle of lives. He leads me into his consciousness and it is there underfoot and all about me. How can I ever lead him into mine?

I have come to a decision. The language I shall teach the Child is the language of these people I have come among, and not after all my own. And in making that decision I know I have made another. I shall never go back to Rome.

No doubt I will go on writing to my wife and my attorney. I shall even go on addressing Augustus, begging him to forgive my crimes and recall me. Because in one-half of my life that is what is expected of me, it is the drama I must play out to its conclusion. But in the other half of my life I know that if the letter came, recalling me, I would not go. More and more in these last weeks I have come to realize that this place is the true destination I have been seeking, and that my life here, however painful, is my true fate, the one I have spent my whole existence trying to escape. We barely recognize the annunciation when it comes, declaring: *Here is the life you have tried to throw away. Here is your second chance. Here is the destiny you have tried to shake off by inventing a hundred false roles, a hundred false identities for yourself. It will look at first like disaster, but is really good fortune in disguise, since fate too knows how to follow your evasions through a hundred forms of its own. Now you will become at last the one you intended to be.*

So I admit openly to myself what I have long known in my heart. I belong to this place now. I have made it mine. I am entering the dimensions of my self.

How all this has begun to happen is a mystery to me. It begins at first, perhaps, in our dreams. Some other being that we have kept out of mind, whose thoughts we have never allowed to come to the tip of our tongue, stirs and in its own way begins to act in us. A whole hidden life comes flooding back to consciousness. So it is that my childhood has begun to return to me. Not as I had previously remembered it, but in some clearer form, as it really was; which is why my past, as I recall it now, continually astonishes me. It is as if it had happened to someone else, and I were being handed a new past, that leads, as I follow it out, to a present in which I appear out of my old body as a new and other self.

So too, in my lessons with the Child. When I try to articulate what I know, I stumble suddenly on what, till that moment, I did not know. There are times when it comes strongly upon me that *he* is the teacher, and that whatever comes new to the occasion is being led slowly, painfully, out of *me*.

We are moving in opposite directions, I and the Child, though on the same path. He has not yet captured his individual soul out of the universe about him. His self is outside him, its energy distributed among the beasts and birds whose life he shares, among leaves, water, grasses, clouds, thunder—whose existence he can be at home in because they hold, each of them, some particle of his spirit. He has no notion of the otherness of things.

I try to precipitate myself into his consciousness of the world, his consciousness of me, but fail. My mind cannot contain him. I try to imagine the sky with all its constellations, the Dog, the Bear, the Dragon and so on, as an extension of myself, as part of my further being. But my knowing that it is sky, that the stars have names and a history, prevents my being the sky. It rains and I say, *it rains.* It thunders and I say, *it thunders.* The Child is otherwise. I try to think as he must: *I am raining, I am thundering,* and am immediately struck with panic, as if, in losing hold of my separate and individual soul, in shaking the last of it off from the tip of my little finger, I might find myself lost out there in the multiplicity of things, and never get back.

But I know now that this is the way. Slowly I begin the final metamorphosis. I must drive out my old self and let the universe in. The creatures will come creeping back—not as gods transmogrified, but as themselves. Beaked, furred, fanged, tusked, clawed, hooved, snouted, they will settle in us, re-entering their old lives deep in our consciousness. And after them, the plants, also themselves. Then we shall begin to take back into ourselves the lakes, the rivers, the oceans of the earth, its plains, its forested crags with their leaps of snow. Then little by little, the firmament. The spirit of things will migrate back into us. We shall be whole.

Only then will we have some vision of our true body as men.

So day by day, as I teach the Child to put sounds

together and make words such as men use, he teaches me to make the sounds of the birds and beasts.

At first it was a game I allowed to humor him. My self-consciousness, the awkwardness of my attempts, made him laugh, and that in itself, the sudden breaking out of the child in him, delighted me, and the notion that we were both playing the same game made it easier for me to keep him involved in the long, slow, difficult task I have set him.

But he, in fact, is the more patient teacher. He shows me the bird whose cry I am trying to imitate. He makes me hold it, trembling in my hands. I know what he intends. I am to imagine myself into its life. As the small, soft creature beats its warmth into me, I close my human mind and try to grow a beak, try to leap up out of myself, defying the heaviness of my own flesh, the solid bones, and imagine what it is to soar out of the wet grass towards the clouds. A strange piping comes from my throat, small bird cries, and the Child clasps his hands and makes the sound himself, encouraging me, bringing me closer to it, the simple scale that is the bird's individual being.

And it is true. Each day brings me closer. Once, in the early days of my desolation, I thought I might learn to write in the language of the spiders. Now, led by the Child, I am on my way to it. The true language, I know now, is that speech in silence in which we first communicated, the Child and I, in the forest, when I was asleep. It is the language I used with him in my childhood, and some memory, intangibly there but not quite audible, of our marvelous conversations, comes to me again at the very edge of sleep, a language my tongue

97

almost rediscovers and which would, I believe, reveal the secrets of the universe to me. When I think of my exile now it is from the universe. When I think of the tongue that has been taken away from me, it is some earlier and more universal language than our Latin, subtle as it undoubtedly is. Latin is a language for distinctions, every ending defines and divides. The language I am speaking of now, that I am almost speaking, is a language whose every syllable is a gesture of reconciliation. We knew that language once. I spoke it in my childhood. We must discover it again.

The season begins to change. Already when we go out these days, to our island in the swamp, I have to wrap up against the wind, which for nearly a month now has blown steadily from the north, though the Child still goes naked, and seems unaffected either by wind or cold. Shadows gather out of the scrub earlier and earlier each day. The light is grayish. The birds who have been our companions out there begin to flock away. Each day there are fewer of them and at dusk, making our way back across the flat watery landscape, we hear the geese flocking south, great waves of them beating across the sky and filling the heights with their honking cry. The beasts have crawled away into the earth to sleep. I feel a slowing in the Child also, and half believe that the secret of his winter survival will be revealed at last. One morning I shall find that he too has taken himself away into some deeper sleep, like the one that filled those first three days after we found him.

Meanwhile the village is being turned into a fort.

Men are out in groups repairing the stockade. The last of the harvest has been brought in and garnered. The byres that are open and empty all summer are being stocked with feed, and in a few weeks now, the beasts will be led in, the oxen, cows, asses, goats, to be stabled under the rooms where we sleep, and when I climb down in the morning there will be their warm breath in the darkness there, the smell of their stale, the sound of their nuzzling and feeding. The yard is piled high with stacks of square-cut peat, and wagons laden with it rumble up the lanes between the huts, with men— or more often half-naked children—yelling and switching the oxen to encourage them uphill through the oozing mud. We are preparing to shut ourselves in. Against the horsemen from the north, who will surely appear again as the river freezes, and against the wolves. In each one of us there is this sense of withdrawal into ourselves, this retirement into the body's secret light and warmth, out of the coming cold; this moving further into some deep inner self that must remain untouched by the closeness that will be forced upon us in these winter months, when first the town is shut up, then our houses, and except for snatches of duty on the walls, we will spend the days and nights equally, huddled together above the one peat stove in the big central room over the byre. Winter here is a time of slow-smoldering resentments, of suspicion, of fantasies that grow as the days move deeper into the year's darkness and the cold drives us closer together and yet further apart.

I am anxious, especially, for the Child. Up till now we have lived apart from the family in my summer outhouse, not quite separate, since the room adjoins the main sleeping rooms of the hut, but able at least to come and go as we please and to see as little of the others as the smallness of our compound allows. I realize, now, how much in these last weeks I have cut myself off, how much I have made my life with the Child the entire limits of my world. Now all that is at an end. My little outhouse will be turned over to the spiders. A week after the first snow it will be all but buried. How will the Child endure our being cooped up in a single room? Will the women, and the boy, accept him?

I mention my anxieties to old Ryzak as we sit, in the late light of the courtyard, over a game these people play with a wooden tablet and pegs.

He is winning as usual, and trying, with his down-drawn mouth and moustache, which he strokes with a stubby forefinger, not to look pleased with himself, though I am too poor a player to offer much challenge. He pretends to find a puzzle where there is none, wags his finger at me, and makes his move.

"No no, my friend, you must trust me. They will not trouble the boy."

But I am not convinced. I am inclined to think that for all his position as headman, and for all his quiet assumption of authority, Ryzak holds less sway over the village than he would have me believe, and less sway, also, over the house. Behind his male preroga-tive, established in law, lies the darker power of the women. The old woman his mother, especially, has a strange ascendancy over him. He shouts at her, and once or twice I have seen him strike her. But his spirit quails before hers, I feel it. In some darker area of belief, it is her demons, the old spirits she mutters to under her breath and sacrifices to by moonlight, who are the powerful beings of this world, and Ryzak knows it. He is scared of her magic, as he is scared also of the shaman. All he has on his side is bodily strength and the authority, such as it is, of the law.

The old woman remains hostile and suspicious. I watch her lips move as she ladles our gruel into bowls, and wonder whether she is simply talking to herself or muttering spells. She has a great reputation in the village as a worker of enchantments, and scarcely a day passes without the village women calling to consult with her on the question of a strawberry mark, or a harelip, or a difficult birth. I have even, on one or two occasions, seen a young man come lurking about, shifting from foot to foot at the gate as he prepares to submit himself to the dangerous world of women's magic. Seeking no doubt a love philter or a charm against mildew or the early dropping of his lambs. She is sometimes to be glimpsed, when we got out to our island, gathering herbs among the wormwood scrub or reading messages out of places in a field where the grass forms circles made neither by beast nor man. I know that she spies on me. She believes, I think, that I am some sort of rival wizard—is that what poet means to her?—who is using the Child to make a different and more potent magic. Her mutterings over our gruel are meant to sing the goodness out of the grains, so that our spirits will find no nourishment in them. But she is too wary of her son to practice directly against us.

Her ally in all this is the boy, Lullo. He is jealous, I

know, because he has been replaced as my pupil—though I have several times offered to return to our lessons. He refuses to come near me, and proclaims loudly that he has no use for Latin or for the simple mathematics I have tried to teach him.

The old man looks rueful. He would like his grandson to acquire these accomplishments but cannot, out of pride, allow any suggestion of his own deficiency. Silently, with his leathery features puckered up in an expression of clownish apology and helplessly affronted dignity, he begs me not to be insulted by the boy's impudence, to sympathize, if I can, with his difficulty. He tells Lullo he is a lout, and cuffs his ear; but gently, and with the suggestion that in choosing loutishness, he is remaining loyal to his own people, and especially, to his uncivilized but unloutish grandfather. The boy accepts the blow as it is intended, with a superior smile in my direction, and swaggers off.

Ryzak shakes his head, makes a mouth, shows me the palms of his hands. The old woman, magnificently justified, celebrates my defeat with a squawk of triumph, and scuttles off to prepare an infusion of herbs in boiled water which she serves with a pantomime of such insolent and exaggerated politeness that Ryzak feels bound to declare the tea undrinkable, and tosses the bowls and their contents into the yard.

Only the boy's mother is too good-natured to have turned entirely against me. She has always considered me some sort of fool whose masculine weakness she ought to indulge. Her humorous affection goes back to my earliest days here, when she tried to teach me the names of the seeds she was sorting; and since she is afraid of the old woman, she is glad of my presence because I am a thorn in the old crone's side. It is she who brings the water for my little plants. It is, I recognize, the subversive act of one who also exists in this house by a sort of uneasy tolerance and who sees in me another like herself.

She comes from a distant village and is of a different race. Her only real hold on this house, now that her husband is dead, is through her son. Or rather, it would be, if Ryzak were not so inordinately fond of her. The old woman, no doubt, puts this down as another mark against him, another of those little softnesses that weaken the structure of things.

It is, perhaps, a similar weakness that makes the young woman, despite the old woman's warnings and her own fear, reach out sometimes and touch the Child as he is stooped over one of his tasks. Softly, and for the merest second, drawn by curiosity, or tenderness, or some impulse to put herself in contact with whatever force it is that is compacted in him, she strokes his hair, starting back the moment he feels her hand. But for that moment, brief as it is, the look on their faces is extraordinary.

I mean to say only that our lives here, even in separation, are alive with tension. And the winter has just begun.

All day today there has been that peculiar stillness in the air, that sickly greenish light that promises snow. Huge curdled clouds over the sea. The animals, who have already been brought indoors, are restless in their stalls, stamping and smoking, or shifting together in the dark. The Child too has been unwilling to settle to our tasks. Like any boy of his age, he can be difficult, and is forever on the lookout for excuses—a kingfisher's wing in the swamp, a grub crawling over a log—to divert my attention. But today it is different. All his muscles remain tense, alert, as if he heard a footfall in the grass behind us. He cannot settle his mind on things, and once or twice he shows little bursts of temper, impatiently pushing my hand away and cocking his head as if the language I am trying to teach him were blocking out another that his ears must be especially sharp to catch.

He is often attuned like this to the shifts of weather. He can smell a change of wind hours before the first breath of it shivers the sea or lifts the marram grass of the swamp. I see him abruptly sit upright in the yard, lift his head, as if at a sudden presence, and know that outside the grass-blades will be swaying in the first cool gust of a new wind, or that the first flickers of lightning will be at play far off on the northern skyline.

But today it is the snow, which we have been expecting now for nearly three weeks. In the fort they are making final preparations. All over the flat gray land the stillness vibrates as if a string had been struck. Everything hums in sympathy.

Sometime between midnight and dawn I am woken by a strange light in the room, an unnatural blue that pulses, not at all like moonlight. The door to the hut is open, and the Child's place in the corner is empty. I get up quickly, and am struck with fear.

But he has not run away. In all that dazzle of light off the snow that must have been falling for hours it is so deep, he is standing naked in the yard (he sleeps naked, even now, when the rest of us have to wrap up in fur) and seems to me to be asleep still—he has that remote entranced look of sleepwalkers, who even when they pass you in a corridor, or on stairs, seem untouchably beyond reach, as if they were moving in some other and equally present world that is separated from ours, but not by walls. He stands perfectly still, with his face raised to the sky, which is of an incandescent blueness, neither of night nor of day, a blueness that sings, it is so clear, so pure, so absolutely its own color.

He stands like that, still in the cold, with the light striking up off the snow, for nearly an hour. I am too scared to wake him. Then when the first light flakes begin to fall again, he opens his mouth to them, rubs his face, his shoulders, his torso, then holds his arms out and his head up so that the light falls directly upon them.

I make a little sound, of shuffling perhaps, since I too have been standing still in the cold, afraid to move lest I disturb him.

He turns and is suddenly awake. Smiles. Lets out a whoop. And begins leaping about in the snow, throwing handfuls of it into the air. He seems unaware of the cold. His body keeps its color, his hands and feet are unnumbed. When he comes scrambling towards me with a handful of crushed snow I can feel the warmth he is giving out, his body glows, he is a furnace. He shows me the snow as if it were something out of his own world that I might never have seen.

But when I try to draw him back into the room he resists. I have never known him so suddenly recalcitrant. I make the mistake of insisting, and he lashes out at me, spitting, tearing at my cloak, and runs to the wall of the stockade, scratching at the raw timber in his attempt to scale it. When I try to calm him he hurls me off and begins to howl. It is the old howling from his days in the forest. He howls, scratching at the wall like an animal, spitting whenever I approach, showing me his teeth and his hands with all the fingers tense and extended like claws. Behind me, the women. And Ryzak, looking alarmed. And the sleepy boy, with his eyes wide open as if one of the old man's stories had suddenly come alive in the yard.

I am on the edge of tears. There is nothing to be done. I wait, with Ryzak, for the Child to exhaust himself. He sinks against the wall at last, with his nails bloody, and I am filled with pity for him, and with a terrible feeling suddenly of guilt; but I cannot touch him. All these weeks I have been following my own plan for the Child, and have never for one moment thought of him as anything but a creature of my will, a figure in my dream. Now, as he kneels in the snow, howling, tearing his face with his nails, I have a vision of his utter separateness that terrifies me. I have no notion of what pain it is he is suffering, what deep sense of loss and deprivation his cries articulate. At last when the howling has subsided to a weak and childlike sobbing, we carry him to his pallet and I huddle at his side, with the door closed, in the dark, till he has sobbed himself asleep.

In the morning he seems to have no memory of the night's events. He watches from his corner while I roll up my bedding, pack my writing materials, my razor and bowl, preparing for a season to abandon this space that is mine—ours—for the common room over the byre. I assure him with gestures that I am not leaving without him and encourage him to get his own things together, such as they are: the rough gown he refuses to wear, his colored ball. But he seems unable to wake properly. He watches while I sweep out the room and, saying good-bye to the spiders, bar the door behind me. By the end of the week snow will have buried our hut, and after that, when it freezes, there will be no getting back inside save through the roof.

Slowly, with all our belongings, we climb the ladder inside the byre to the upper room.

IV

OUR winter dream begins.

It is my fifth year in this place, and I have still not grown used to it. Day in day out there is the same grayish light over the marshes, it snows, freezes, snows again, the wind blows steadily off the steppes. Inside our room the air is thick with smoke from the peat that smolders under us. The windows are kept barred for the most part against the wind, and can be opened only on those strange still days of absolute frost when the sky turns icy blue and the whole world holds its breath and glitters blue, gold, white, as if we had suddenly stepped through into a new land. Otherwise we huddle here in the half-dark, listening to the wind whistle around the eaves, shaking clumps of snow down with a heavy thump; listening to the wooden shutters rattle and the icicles clink, and protecting ourselves against the draughts that find their way in and blow up little eddies in the smoke-filled air. I write by a guttering candle, having to shield it, every now and then, with a cupped hand, to protect its being sucked out by a sudden gust. For a good deal of the time I sleep. It may be the heaviness of the air, or some slowing of the blood in the extreme cold, or perhaps it is simply boredom, but I find myself nodding off at odd hours of the day and seem always drowsy and thick-headed. How many hours a day, I wonder, do I spend half sleeping, half dreaming? Twelve, fifteen?

The days, with so little to mark one off from another, pass quickly, falling away into absolute oblivion like the nights. A week passes, three weeks, five. Unless one notches them off on a stick, or marks them on parchment, one hardly knows they have been and gone.

I measure the weeks by how many guard duties I have done. One night in five I go out for four hours and man the wall, pacing up and down on a wooden parapet, just below the spiked summit of the palisade, with twenty others. On clear nights it can be beautiful: the moon high among clouds, the river flats bluish, broken with thick shadow, the whole countryside open as far as the eye can see, all the way to the river. On such watches you can see the wolves moving in packs over the snow, and if it is still enough, hear them howling. Sometimes a lone wolf will come right up to the wall, and once or twice a whole pack will appear, showing their fangs in the moonlight and filling the air with their terrible yowling, as they smell the beasts in their stalls, and the oxen, the asses, hearing their howls, make their own uneasy bellowing and braying in return. But most nights we just pass up and down in the fog that swirls around us like the sea, moving like blindmen with one hand extended before us on the narrow walk. The four hours then are like another kind of sleep. There is nothing for the eye to fix on and every sound is dampened. It is gray, dreamless sleep, that makes the knees ache and tightens the skull, and I have the greatest difficulty preventing myself then from falling into real sleep, and may be plummeting twelve meters into frozen mud.

The Child meanwhile has fallen into a state of apathy in which he sits for hours simply staring into the gloom, his elbows round his knees, his chin sunk on his clenched fists. He still quickens at moments, cocking his head for the rising of the wind after a lull or sniffing suddenly as the snow clouds move in upon us; and in the breaks of brilliant stillness when the windows can be opened, he becomes almost crazy with joy, rocking on his heels at the edge of the sill, and making little whimpering sounds like a puppy that has been let off the leash. But in the long periods when we are closed in by fog or snow, or by the severity of the frost, he sinks back into his old sullenness, and nothing will call him out of it. He feeds if the food is set in front of him. But he shows no interest now in our speech games, and I fear he will forget most of what we have learned. Once, when I tried to engage him again by making one of the calls he had been teaching me, he became quite hysterical. All that my futile attempt at a birdcall had done was remind him of the place in the swamp that we have not visited now for three months or more, and I realize, painfully, that he does not understand, cannot understand, why we no longer go there or why our games have ended. Does he think I am punishing him?

One clear night, when we opened the windows, he tried to throw himself out, and I had to wrestle with him at the sill, while he kicked and uttered the raucous animallike cries that have once again convinced the old woman that he is no child but a beast in disguise who has wheedled his way in among us.

She watches him continually. She is terrified, I think, that he may touch something, some utensil, and thereby gain power over its users. And it is true that in his long hours of simply sitting, staring before him, he seems in no way like a normal child; and when he growls in his throat, or whimpers or makes little yelping sounds in his pain, even I begin to wonder if some animal spirit does not occasionally come creeping back into him—some spirit that succored him out there in the winter forest. He survived then. Can he survive now? I watch him retreat further each day into some invisible distance, some secret lair, where his spirit slumbers and cannot be recalled.

Looking at him on occasions, I have a clear glimpse of what he is doing. He is dreaming himself out into the winter countryside. I see him, briefly, moving over the soft snow among the birch trees, chewing strips of bark, kneeling to tear up lichen. I touch his shoulder, and he feels nothing. The black eyes, sunk deep in their sockets, stare through me, to dazzling fields of ice under the wind. When he quickens to a change of weather, it is, I realize now, to the change that comes over a landscape he is moving through in his head. If I thought we might find him again in the spring, I would let him go. But that is impossible. Having brought him in among us there is no way back. Already, in the warmth of the room, he is losing his capacity to withstand cold. For weeks now he has wrapped himself, like the rest of us, in a blanket of hide. Out there he would freeze. Whatever his secret was, I have taken it from him. He is as vulnerable now as anyone of us, and in that at least—even if the old woman does not see it—he shows himself human at last.

As if to prove what I have just perceived, the Child has a fever. Sitting as he does with his knees drawn up, staring, he suddenly pitches over and lies in a faint, but when I move to cover him, he wakes, and almost immediately begins shivering. Huge beads of sweat break out on his brow, his hair drips with it, his whole body streams. And in between the periods of burning, he freezes. I think he has never known before what it is to be cold. His whole body clenches on it, this new feeling, this discovery within himself of what winter means, what it is to be snow and ice, to feel oneself enter the realm of absolute cold, that polar world at the body's limits. He draws his knees up, closing upon himself. Every muscle in his limbs, his shoulders, his neck, goes rigid, his fists clench, his jaws tighten. He looks terrified, and when the convulsions begin I have to hold him, forcing a knife handle between his teeth, while he jerks, stiffens, goes through a whole series of spasms, and then sinks exhausted into a kind of nerveless sleep. Then again, the sweating. As I raise him in my arms and try to force a few drops of water between his lips, I am reminded of my brother, and realize what he means to me this Child, what it might mean to lose him.

The old woman watches from across the room. I know what she is thinking. This is no ordinary fever. The Child is wrestling with his demon, the animal spirit who protected him out there in the forest, and is fighting now to get back. When I appeal to her for some sort of medicine, some of the herbs she gathers and makes potions of, she shakes her head and turns her thumb down, spitting. I have to watch the Child day and night. If she thought for even a moment that the spirit might triumph and enter the Child's body again, she would cut his throat. I know it.

But the younger woman, who has a child of her own and is softhearted, cannot bear to see the boy writhe as he does, and sweat, and shiver, and jerk about under the rugs. Secretly she brings me food for him and a bowl of clean water.

I hear the old woman arguing with her, and I know what she is saying. What if the Child gave up the struggle, and we found ourselves shut up here with the giant white wolf who is his familiar, and who might at any moment succeed in filling the Child's body and then breaking out of it. The fever, she believes, is part of the painful transformation. The Child's blood boils and freezes, as drop by drop it is being changed. The Child's belly cringes for the raw meat that is the wolf's diet. His limbs strain to grow claws. His jaw clenches against the growing there of fangs. And what if it isn't a wolf after all? But some other beast? Larger, more terrible than even she can imagine.

The young woman quails. And I see a new doubt has been sown in her mind. What if the beast, finding the Child too difficult to conquer, chose the body of her own son instead? It would be so easy. While we are all sleeping, our bodies empty in the dark, the Child's spirit slips out, crosses the room, enters her son's body —and there, it is done!

For two whole days the young woman refuses to come near us. She watches the Child, she watches her son, she keeps the boy as far from our corner of the room as possible, while the old woman whispers and flaps about between us.

But in the dead of night, when the Child's fever is at its crisis, and I am forced to call for help, it is the younger woman who stirs in the dark, wraps herself in her cloak, and comes with water. I am desperately tired and through sheer exhaustion, after nearly five days of watching, seem always on the edge of tears. My hand shakes so much that I cannot lift the bowl to the Child's lips.

She takes it from me. Kneels. Lifts the boy's head, letting him gulp at the coolness, and when she has laid his head back on the pile of rags I have contrived for a pillow, sits fanning him, while I rest for a moment against the wall and sleep. When I start awake again she is still there, her face just visible in the folds of the cloak. She sits perfectly upright, her hand moving back and forth to make a breeze. She nods, indicating that I may sleep again, and immediately I fall back into my body's depths.

In the early morning light that seeps in through the window cracks, I wake to find her holding the Child in one of his fits. She looks frightened, and I know that this is the real moment of crisis. I know too what it is she fears.

The Child's body jerks, loosens, his limbs fly about,

his jaws clench and unclench, strange animal sounds come from them. I hear the others begin to stir, and see the old woman come out of the darkness to watch, and the boy rising sleepily behind her. The Child grunts, low growls come from his throat. His tongue lolls and saliva rolls from the corner of his mouth. His lips move. And suddenly, so clearly that we all hear it—I and the young woman, who suddenly gasps and pushes him from her, the old woman who lets out a howl—clearly, from his lips, among all the growling and whines of animal pain, comes a word, one of the words I have been trying all these weeks to teach him. He has discovered it at last in his delirium. It has come to the surface of his mind. His tongue has discovered how to produce it.

It is quite an ordinary word, and has no significance. Just one of the common words of this people's daily life. But the effect on them is immediate. And in my joy at his discovering his humanity at last I fail to see what it is that alarms them. The young woman stumbles to her feet, terrified, and begins to back away. The old woman reaches a hand out to take her, and another behind to catch the boy. They huddle together with the boy between them, staring, while I look up from the floor at the Child's side, unable for the moment to comprehend.

It is what the old woman has predicted. In the depths of his fever, at the crisis point, the Child has snatched away another soul. His suddenly speaking out like that, a word in their own language, proves it.

It is the boy Lullo they now turn to, since it is he who has, without knowing it, spoken from the Child's mouth. The old woman immediately begins wailing over him, cursing the younger woman who has deserted her own child to care for an interloper, and in nursing him up to the crisis has made it possible for the demon to steal, if only for a moment, her son's spirit. The younger woman is speechless with fear. She staggers about the rushes, holding her belly and making little wordless sounds in her throat as if she might be about to be sick. The boy begins to whimper, and the old woman tears his clothes off to search his body for marks, signs, some place where the demon may have got in. An hour later, when Ryzak returns from guard duty, the room is in utter turmoil. Both women are hysterical and the boy is laid out on his pallet, sweating in the first onset of fever, while the Child, his own crisis over at last, breathes quietly and sleeps.

My mind is awhirl with all this.

At any other moment I might be overjoyed at what has occurred. The Child has spoken at last. In his delirium he has discovered human speech. The first step has been taken that will lead him inevitably now into the world of men. If this had happened six or seven weeks ago, out there in the marshes, I would be beside myself with joy. Now I am aware only of the danger he has put himself in. That first human word, drawn up out of the depths of himself in sleep, while his mind perhaps, his spirit, was far off in the deep snow of his forest, may destroy him.

He is innocent of all danger, his breath coming softly between his lips now as he sleeps; but the danger is real, and I dare not leave him, or allow myself to fall, even for a moment, into my own body's hunger for rest. In their corner opposite, too occupied for the moment to pay us any attention, the two women are wailing over the body of the boy, whose moans can be heard, lightly, between the spaces of their howling. He is in the early stages of the same sickness the Child had. I recognize the symptoms.

How did he take it?

What comes to my mind is the look of alarm on the boy's face, the terror of some unknown presence, as the old woman's hands tore at him, searching his body for signs of invasion. Did he take the disease then? Catching her fear and making it his own? Who knows by what mysterious means the body moves to its ends? Years ago, on my travels in Asia Minor, I came upon a city that was visited by plague. What struck me then was the randomness with which the disease advanced, how it appeared in one house, striking down all but a single child, who remained quite unscathed, then leapt two houses to claim another victim. I came to believe then that as well as the plague itself, moving like a cloud over the city, there must also be some shadow of the plague that lives in the body or in the mind, and that only when the two meet and recognize one another can the disease break in. How else explain why one man takes it and another, sitting beside him, or sleeping in the same bed, does not? And what can that shadow be, that sleeps there in the body, but fear? It is terror that is the link. The body breaks into a sweat of fear, and in the dampness of that sweat, the plague begins to swarm, each drop is transformed and becomes fever sweat. What begins in the mind works now upon the body. So too, once, I saw the disease transmitted in the theater. A famous actor at Antioch, portraying the last anguish of a hero who had been stricken with a deadly fever, after insulting the gods, worked so powerfully upon the minds of the audience, reproduced so perfectly the burning, the choking, the paroxysms of the disease, that half a dozen spectators, out of their own terror, their own guilt, suddenly fell ill with it, dropped sweating from their seats, and had to be carried out. Their minds had so taken the impression of what they saw that the mere simulation of the disease, in the actor's body, had communicated itself to their bodies and become real. The actor's spirit, in imagining the disease, had so powerfully affected theirs that they had let the illness in, and immediately all its poisons flooded through their veins.

Is that how such fevers spread? Is that how the boy has been afflicted? Not through some wish of the Child's to free himself by passing the disease on, but through fear, carried in the mind of his mother, imprinted upon his own mind by the old woman's sudden panic, and immediately translating itself into sweat, into fire, into the fits he is now enduring. The point of infection was that moment when the old woman reached out her hand to touch the young woman, as she started away in terror at the Child's speaking, and turned with a cry towards the sleepy child behind her. In this first shock at the old woman's scream, he took the disease, his body opened to receive it from her hands, through his mother's from the Child. Out of their mind into his. Though what the old woman believes, and has impressed upon the younger, is that the Child's spirit has worked all this out of malice, and that the boy's mother has indeed been made the carrier, but through her own weakness and pity. In turning aside to care for the Child she has betrayed her son's life to him. She has permitted the death spirit to pass between them.

So hourly, the boy Lullo sinks deeper into delirium, shouting, muttering, allowing through his lips the same whimpering cries and growls of animal pain that the Child has filled the room with all this last week, and wrestling, so the women believe, with the same animal spirit, which will use him to gain entry among us. Meanwhile the Child, unaware of all this, grows stronger. Today he sits up, too weak to support himself as yet, but strong enough to eat again. And smiles.

Even Ryzak now regards the Child's return to health with narrow eyes, and I see in him some real fear of what the Child may have done to them, though like the women he is too anxious, too torn with grief at his grandson's suffering, to do more than stare and wonder. His feelings are entirely engaged with the small, pale figure on the rushes, who clasps his hand in fit after fit as the fever moves through its phases of fire and ice. It is only when the illness has done with him at last that the old man's sense of shock will turn to resentment, to anger against us. For five days and nights he squats on the floor at the child's side, his shoulders hunched, his face set, the tears occasionally, as the boy whimpers, wetting his cheeks. I know what he feels but can make no move towards him. I try to make myself invisible here, and take the Child with me. The young woman, the boy's mother, is too stunned now, with grief, with guilt, to do more than sit with her head covered, staring at the boy, willing him back to life. It is the old woman who tends him. Should the boy die, I know, all this fierce emotion that surrounds us will break out into violence. There will be nothing I can do then to protect the Child or myself. Half dozing, I wait for the moment when it will come —the hoarse cry of rage that will tear through the old man and come hurtling upon us, the violence that, shaking the boy now, will come raging through the old man's body to strike back at us, at the Child first, and then surely, if I try to protect him, at me.

But miraculously the fifth night passes, and the boy survives. As morning comes I hear the old woman make little clucking sounds, talking to the boy as if he could hear at last and shaking Ryzak out of the half-sleep he has fallen into, his head dropped forward, though his body, as he squats, is perfectly upright. The boy's mother rises slowly to her feet, out of the place against the wall where for five days now she has been sunk in abject seclusion. Ryzak clasps his hands and utters big shouts of boisterous relief, teasing the boy, I guess, for giving them all so much worry, and he immediately comes to the middle of the room, grinning, and waves his hand at me. All his fear and resentment have vanished. He crosses to the window and lifts the bar. Bright light floods the room. It is one of those clear white days when the whole countryside is visible, glittering white under a sky of cloudless blue, and the sudden rush of cold air into the room is extraordinary. Ryzak stretches, utters another huge shout as he holds his arms out wide to the sky, and then, staggering back into the room, rolls into the pile of rushes that is his bed and immediately falls into the first real sleep he has known for nearly a week. The boy's mother also sleeps, stretched out on the floor at his side. Only the old woman, who is tireless, continues to crow over the child, offering him tidbits from a plate, occasionally laughing to herself, even once or twice calling across to me, though what she is saying in her toothlessness I can never tell.

The danger is past. We have come through. Suddenly I remember how tired I am. A great wave comes over me, and without even crawling the three feet to my bed of rushes, I allow myself to sink back under the flood of light from the window and sleep.

We are already past the worst of it. The winter solstice has long since come and gone, the dark of the year's deepest place has been entered and the limit touched, the earth swings away towards the light again, and I feel my own spirits lifted as the days begin to lengthen. More and more often now periods of still bright weather open the whole country to our view, the sea glitters, the first birds return, the ice of the river on still nights can be heard grinding in the dark.

We can even begin at last to move about the house. I go down with the Child to the byre and we sit there with the animals, hearing them snuffle and snort in the half-dark, shifting, chewing, dropping the steaming heaps of dung that give the place its acrid odor, which seems almost pleasant after the stale air of the upper room, feeling their warmth as they crowd together in their stalls. They begin to be restless, scenting the spring. In two or three weeks now, when the ice has been cleared away, they will be led out into the fields again. Each day men are at work, chopping corridors through the ice, digging away the feet of frozen snow that block the narrow lanes between the huts, clearing yards to make outhouses accessible again. Even my own little house begins to reappear above the level of the snow. Soon we will be able to move back there, the Child and I, and our old life will resume. Then in a month or so we will return to our island in the swamp, to the birds, the moths, the new spring caterpillars, the vowels and consonants the Child has almost forgotten, it is so long since we rehearsed them; though now that he has spoken a word at last I know they are still to be found there at the bottom of his mind, that in some secret part of his being, deeper even than sleep, he has begun to speak to himself, and will eventually speak to me.

We go down each day to the byre because the room itself has become intolerable. We exist there only on sufferance. Only because Ryzak is responsible for me.

His power over the household has been deeply shaken by the events of the last weeks. It is the old woman who rules. It was her magic that saved the boy's life—this is what she tells him—and his foolish trust, and the young woman's pity, that exposed them all to destruction. The boy is, after all, his only grandson. When he watches him now it is with a quickened sense of how vulnerable the child is, how vulnerable *he* is, to extinction, and with some realization also of how little his strength of arms can do, and did do, at the moment of crisis. It is as if the old woman had found a way at last of poisoning his spirit, of stealing back the male strength she once gave him and which all these years has been the source of his ascendancy over her. There are moments when he seems almost like a child in her presence. One recognizes in the old woman's face real hostility to this sixty-year-old man who has been her master for so long, and was once a suckling, utterly in her power. And mixed with hostility, a new sense of triumph. The house is filled with the glow of her magic, the smell of her herbs, her potions and the endless doddering syllables of her prayers.

At the first full moon she will sacrifice in the women's grove outside the village, in thanksgiving for the boy's life. Ryzak goes out alone to bring back the victim, a wild puppy, whose entrails will be burned on an altar of turf and offered up to the triple Hecate. The boy begs to go with him but is refused. The puppy will be taken from among the wild dogs, part mongrel, part wolf, that roam in packs through the undergrowth beyond the village and are, on occasion, since they are also sacred, fed scraps from the parapets. Lean, gray-black creatures, all ribs, they fight, tumbling in heaps over their strips of meat and rancid fat, then slink into the brush.

Ryzak returns with the puppy in a little wicker basket, and for ten days, until the full moon, it whimpers in a corner of the room, and is a source of real agony to the Child. Waking in the dark, to hear the soft crying, I have thought it was the Child himself, and finding him crouched over the basket in the dark, answering the animal's cries with little high-pitched whinings of his own, have had the greatest difficulty drawing him back to his pallet. And all the time I was aware of the old woman, sitting bolt upright in her corner, watching, and have imagined her invisible smile.

Does the Child know what is intended? Has she had the small creature brought here deliberately, and early, only to establish this communication between them, the Child and her animal victim? Is the ceremony she is preparing less an offering of thanks for the life of the boy than an exorcism of the Child?

As the time approaches the Child becomes more and more agitated and I fear he may relapse into his fever. The merest sound from the puppy sets him trembling now, and if I restrain him from going to the basket he will answer the creature from a distance, reproducing absolutely the whole range and pitch of its whinings, and the old woman laughs outright, her savage, crow-like caw. Does the animal sense what is to occur? Does he communicate it to the Child? Or is it simply the presence in the room at last of some kindred spirit, something other than our human presence, that disturbs him? Or some new realization, in the animal's distress, of his own loss of freedom? Or is it, night after night, the growing brightness of the moon? For nearly a week now the weather has been clear, and we sleep with the windows unbarred and the moon's light upon the room, picking out its familiar objects with a ghostly blueness, which is the moonlight striking off snow, and making thick, almost palpable shadows.

At last the night arrives. The two women go out just after the rising of the moon, taking the boy, and Ryzak carries the basket as far as the courtyard gate, then climbs the ladder again and suggests one of our games with the tablet and pegs.

From the window I watch the old woman's party pass along the narrow lane, gathering adherents as it goes. All the women of the village will assemble at last in the grove. No man is permitted to see their rites. These are the offices of the moon, and belong to the world of women's power and women's worship, that are older, more mysterious, than the world of men. Ryzak, as we play, seems oddly ill at ease and I actually win a game. When the women come back they are silent, still wrapped in whatever power it is that the moon has over them, plucking as it does monthly at the tides of their bodies, swelling in them, waning, brooding over the darkness and transmuting all those things that we know by daylight in its softer, vaguer light. Almost immediately, without speaking, Ryzak retires to his pallet. Their silence oppresses him. The Child, who has made no move since the puppy was taken from the room, sits hunched in his corner, deep in one of his body trances, and refuses to sleep. I am aware all night of a strangeness that is upon us, a change, that may be simply the full moon, but seems rather to emanate from the Child's dreamlike wakefulness, or the old woman's, since all night she sits with her eyes wide open, unseeing, and the moon full upon her, taking its power deep into her and uttering, occasionally, great sighs, as if some stronger creature were breathing regularly through her.

In the morning there is a stranger, harsher breathing in the room.

Ryzak has been stricken overnight with some illness,

which is not the same illness the children had. His body buckles and heaves in violent paroxysms, is wrenched, drained, flooded; and when the old woman examines him there is just the mark she expected to find, a half-circle of small teeth marks on his wrist, almost healed now—the wound through which the beast has entered. She utters a piercing shriek, throws her hands in the air, and immediately begins wailing for the dead.

This is what her rites of last evening were intended to avert. They have failed. It wasn't the boy after all who was under threat, but the old man. The boy's illness was a diversion. Now truly, she discovers, the Child has worked his evil upon them. The animal spirit has deserted him at last and entered the old man, from whose lips come flecks of white like the foam on a horse that has been ridden too hard. The savage, animallike growls and roarings that burst from him make the hair stand on end, as hour after hour he writhes, and there bubbles in his throat a low grumbling that is like nothing I have ever heard before, and seems centuries from human speech. Between these passages of frenzy, he stiffens, all his limbs straining against the breaking out through him of whatever beast it is that is coming to birth in him, seeking its four hairy limbs, its fanged snout, its jaws clenched on the raw flesh of things. The end is inevitable, and obviously so from the first moment of the evil's appearance. Even I see that. It is like a nightmare, as if we had all suddenly been swept up into his body's drama, into the terrible process of it, the transfusion of his human energy into its animal form. The nightmare has its own momentum and takes us with it as if we were all participants suddenly in the same dream, waking together in our sleep to discover that the room had become a cage, and the air itself was an animal agency whose breath we shared, whose stench was ours, whose growls were our own choking attempt to cry out and shock ourselves awake.

The shaman is sent for. But even he admits defeat. One look at the gray, wolflike face of the old man and he starts back in horror, shakes his head, flees with his magic before it too is contaminated.

It is all so sudden, so complete, we remain stunned, unable to shake ourselves back to reality. For five days the noise is ceaseless. The old man's spirit wrestles and writhes, his strength seems inexhaustible. When the young woman tries to wet his lips with water, a terrible choking comes from him, as if some new form of speech were trying to burst out at his lips. All the muscles of his throat contract to make the new sound, but nothing comes forth. It is, the old woman screams, the animal attempting to speak its name—the unknown monster who all these years has suckled the Child, and has now left him and is bringing itself to birth again in the old man.

At last on the fifth day he falls quiet, and the sudden stillness after all those hours of frenzy is terrifying. We hold our breath.

He isn't dead. We see that from the rise and fall of his ribs, but the beast now is at a new game. The old woman's eyes dart about, seeking some breath of air in motion about us that would reveal its presence, as on all fours it skulks about the room, so that we almost feel, with the pimpling of our flesh, the touch of its fur upon us as it passes. But there is no sound, no movement. Only the rise and fall of our breathing. The Child clings to me, and seems about to go into some kind of fit of his own. The old woman's eyes continue to prowl the room, her hands held poised in the air, all the fingers spread. Minutes pass. Hours. We are frozen. Too terrified to move.

The rest too is enacted as in a dream: our removal from the room, the coming of the men who will conduct Ryzak's spirit out of the house, my escape with the Child through the roof and down into the darkness of my snowbound summerhouse, from which I listen to what is passing in the yard.

The women of the village, or as many of them as can be crowded in between the paling walls, have gathered there to frighten away the alien spirits who are lurking, just beyond the limits of the house, to snatch the old man's spirit as it passes into the air. Heavily cloaked and veiled, with only their eyes and hands visible in the blackness, they squat in the snow, swaying backward and forward on their haunches and beating together, in earsplitting unison, the sacred stones that have been chosen from the river bed for their whiteness and smoothness, and which are used only for this, to deafen the ears of the evil ones to the old man's cries, so that the last of all, the death cry, will pass unnoticed and his spirit may slip by them in the night.

The clicking begins as a series of short sharp explosions, their spaces filled with a high-pitched wailing and three hawklike shrills. As the rhythms quicken the beats become irregular. But however unexpected the pattern may be to a foreign ear, every stone comes down simultaneously, and as the rhythms open out in an ever increasing sequence, the voices fall to a droning *om om om,* the one original syllable repeated over and over as if the earth itself were speaking out of a chasm with many mouths.

In little earthenware bowls all round the yard some herb is smoking that I have never smelt before. Its fumes in the nostrils leave one dizzy. The whiteness of the walls, the blackness of the figures that fill every available space, the hundred hands moving together, the droning, the crash of pebbles—all this creates a vibration in the head that lulls and then deadens the senses. I find myself being gathered into the expanding and contracting of the light, of the sounds as they strike my ear, as if, in regulating my breath, my heartbeat, to these rhythms, I were slowly being drawn apart and scattered, separated from myself and my individual will.

Upstairs in the house some final ceremony is being performed that we are not permitted to see, and which this confusion of many voices is intended to obscure. I know what it is. The elders of the village are taking Ryzak's life by force, beating and shaking the last breath out of his tough old body so that he will die fighting. For him simply to dwindle into a state of childlike weakness would leave him vulnerable at last to the demons who are hovering there in the darkness to pluck his spirit away. He is being savaged to death. Only in this way can his dying spirit be raised to such a pitch of violence that the dark ones will quail before it and he may pass unharassed on the air.

This goes on for perhaps an hour. Then at last one of the old men appears at a window and raises his arms. Immediately there is silence. The hands stop in mid-gesture, the buzzing cuts out. Only the old woman, Ryzak's mother, raises a long shriek, a single note which she holds to the very end of her breath, when it is taken up by the younger, and they go on thus, striking the note, holding it, changing, while inside, the men begin to dance, stamping on the wooden planks with their booted heels. This is the wake. The village elders will go on dancing and drinking fermented liquor till the last of them has sunk into a stupor like the dead man. Laughing, joking with one another as if no death had occurred, they stagger out into the snow to piss against a wall, so drunk some of them that they can barely stand and have to support themselves with one hand while they fumble to loosen their breeches. Once again, it is the demons of the air who are the object of all this. The old men are diverting their attention while one of their number makes his way to the burial ground, out there on the high plateau. His spirit has already arrived, perhaps, and is riding round the great circle in the dark. Two days from now they will carry the body out to join it. Meanwhile the women huddle in the snow and wait. When the last of the dancers has fallen, they will creep in and remove the dead man so that he can be washed and prepared for impaling.

In the midst of all this it comes to me clearly what I must do. With Ryzak dead, and in such a manner, we have no protection here, I and the Child. For the moment they have forgotten us. The rituals of death, and the preoccupation with the waiting demons, have allowed us to slip quietly away. It is only later, when the last rite has been completed, that someone—the old woman perhaps—will think of vengeance, and remember that it is the Child who has wrought all this, with me as his witting or unwitting familiar.

Just before dawn I wake the Child. The women now are mostly dozing, hunched up together in their black cloaks, their heads covered, and it is easy to creep round them and out into the lane.

The Child is still half-asleep, but when we come to the edge of the marshes and the bridge to our island among the reeds, he suddenly clutches my hand, laughs, gives a little leap, and tries to drag me towards it. After nearly four months he thinks we are about to go back at last to our old life, our daily lessons in the swamp, to the birdcalls, to his fluttering attempts to entice out of the organs of his throat the vowels and consonants that have so long been hidden there and which I am helping him to find. He is disappointed when I make him understand that we must go on.

He looks petulant, pushing out his lower lip, and strikes my chest with his closed fist—not hard, but as an expression of his displeasure with me. He turns away and begins to moan. There is a pallid light over all the swamp with its puddles of turbid water and patches of bluish, moonstruck ice. The reeds hiss. The moon slides in and out of cloud. The Child yearns toward its light on the solid, safe ground behind us, and I have to pluck at his cloak, then at last take his hand and lead him. Something perhaps in my mood warns him that this is no game, and that my refusal to enter the old life is not mere willfulness on my part. He follows, dragging a little, and we start out across the marshes towards the river, which I know lies somewhere to the north, two or three days away as we will have to travel—on foot, and across a terrain that makes heavy going but where we will leave no sign of our passage.

My plan is to cross the river while it is still frozen and escape into the steppes. It is a desperate plan, but I can think of no other. Something deep at the bottom of my mind tells me it is what must be done and has always been intended.

I think of my dreams. Of all those nights when I made my way out there in sleep to scratch in the earth for my own grave. And of that dream of the godlike horsemen. I am going out now into the unknown, the real unknown, compared with which Tomis was but a degenerate outpost of Rome, and am, I believe, following the clear path of my fate. Always to be pushing out like this, beyond what I know cannot be the limits— what else should a man's life be? Especially an old man who has, by a clear stroke of fortune, been violently freed of the comfortable securities that make old men happy to sink into blindness, deafness, the paralysis of all desire, feeling, will. What else should our lives be but a continual series of beginnings, of painful settings out into the unknown, pushing off from the edges of consciousness into the mystery of what we have not yet become, except in dreams that blow in from out there bearing the fragrance of islands we have not yet sighted in our waking hours, as in voyaging sometimes the first blossoming branches of our next landfall come bumping against the keel, even in the dark, whole days before the real land rises to meet us.

I have become braver in my old age, ready at last for all the changes we must undergo, as painfully we allow our limbs to burst into a new form, let the crust of our flesh split and the tree break through, or the moth or bird abandon us for air. What else is death but the refusal any longer to grow and suffer change?

Soft and silly as I may be, I have survived. I am the last poet of our age, existing still, working still, even out here beyond the limits of our speech, even in silence. And if other old men must be willing, at the end, to push up off their deathbed and adventure out into the unknown, how much more willing must that man be whose whole life has been just such a daily exercise of adventuring, even in the stillness of his own garden? I mean, the poet.

So we stumble on, the Child and I, towards that mysterious arc of water whose name I have known all my life as marking the boundaries of our Roman world, and whose syllables *Is-ter* have always given me, even in the days when such notions were the merest romantic indulgence, some thrill in my innermost being that I am at last to make actual. *Is-ter. Is-ter.* It has been there always, somehow waiting, even as my eye noted it on maps, as the final boundary of my life, waiting to be crossed, and patient year after year for my arrival. However many steps I may have taken away from it, both in reality and in my mind, it remained, shifting its tides, freezing each season, cracking up, flowing again, whispering to me: *I am the border beyond which you must go if you are to find your true life, your true death at last.*

Comfortably asleep in my little trundle bed at Sulmo,

the spoiled second son of a rich landowner, how could
I ever have guessed it? What had I to do with this last
river at the end of the known world? Scribbling exotic
romances in a metropolitan garden, overfed, light-
headed with wine and conversation, projecting extravagant fables on the unknown, what need had I to listen
for its rising somewhere deep at the back of my head,
grinding its ice floes, creaking, painfully breaking up
and pushing its thousand miles to the sea? Now at last,
in the early light of a late winter morning, at the very
edge of spring, I make my way towards it through the
dazzling swamp, hauling with me a Child I can never
have expected to find again at this end point of my life,
and stopping, even in the midst of the wide marsh
waters, to listen for it, for the sound of its rumbling
somewhere beyond the horizon there, where the sea-
birds are wheeling.

The time has come at last. Far to the north, deep in
the grasslands that roll away towards the pole, is the
place I have so often dreamed of in these years of my
exile, walking out under the high moonlit clouds in my
sleep. The land I am about to enter is not entirely unfamiliar.

And there, after all these seasons, is the river. *Is-ter.*
Those two magic syllables, born of my own breath
frozen solid, and waiting, in these last days before it
breaks up and flows again, to be crossed. As the Child
and I set out upon it in the moonlight the noise is
deafening, the groaning, the cracking, the grinding of
its whiteness under us. Halfway across, far out in the
glimmering waste of it, we can see nothing, neither the
shore we have left nor the one that lies somewhere

ahead. Till at last, half closing my eyes against the dazzle, I make out the fine, dark horizontal line where the earth declares itself solid again.

Somewhere, in the middle of our crossing, I had the cold fear that there might be no other shore, that Ister might be shoreless on that farther side, a river freezing and flowing at the border between earth and air, and all those stories of the grasslands, and their giant horsemen, the merest figments of our imagination, even when they came thundering over the ice bridge and we held our snowbound fort against them.

But the earth goes on. Even beyond Ister. There is another world out there.

We have come to the shores, and prepare to enter.

V

No more dreams. We have passed beyond them into the last reality.

The grasslands, under the first touch of spring, sway and ripple like the sea, so that wading through them, swimming at times through the chest-high grass heads, is more like floating than walking, with no landmark as far as the eye can see. Above, an immensity of blue sky, and only the smallest, far-off clouds as ceiling.

Back there in the scrublands beyond the river this lack of objects for the eye to focus on seemed like deprivation of the spirit, and I spent my whole time longing for something to break the skyline, one of the slim dark cypresses of my home country, or a chestnut with the sun pouring through it, making every big leaf transparent, a luminous green. Here the immensity, the emptiness, feeds the spirit, and leaves it with no hunger for anything but more space, more light—as if one had suddenly glimpsed the largeness, the emptiness of one's own soul, and come to terms with it, glorying at last in its open freedom.

So one moves here as in another atmosphere. It is as if the very air were different, thinner in the head, as it can be at times on mountaintops. Even my bones seem lighter. And though I am tired almost beyond tiredness by these long days of pushing north into the sky, my body feels almost no ache, only a kind of remoteness from itself. I feel sometimes as if I were moving on two separate planes. I see us as from a great height, two tiny figures parting the grassland with a shadowy crease as we move through it, like swimmers; and from that height the body's tiredness is as nothing. The physical ache is there but it cannot be felt over such a distance, as a cry for example, from so far-off, could not be heard. The spirit experiences what the body does but in a different form. It does not move along a line with the body, northward, dividing the grasses' light. It expands to become the whole landscape, as if space itself were its dimensions; filling the whole land from horizon to horizon and the whole arch of sky, its quality now the purest air, a myriad particles of light, each one a little center from which the whole can be grasped at a single glance, and from whose vantage point, above, I see those tiny figures crawling, who are the Child and myself. From a point far ahead I see us approaching. From a point a whole day's distance behind us, I see us moving away.

At evening big shadows move over the hills, dipping into the hollows and deepening their slopes, which are gentle enough when we come to them. On still days there is only the sound of wings, the clicketing of insects all about us, as they cluster at the grass roots or flicker in the air. When the north wind blows it freezes, and the whole landscape seethes. We crawl in then, like insects, under the roots, and let the great sea roll over us. But when the south wind blows it is warm with the first breath of spring. And already, everywhere about us, are the signs of spring: little wild flowers deep in the grass, grubs that the Child gathers, and which we feed upon, the first of the birds that come flocking back to the ripening grass heads—great clouds of them ballooning in the sky, falling like a low cloud over the uplands, suddenly streaming out before us in a funnel shape as our wading into their universe disturbs them as they feed.

This is the Child's world at last. He plunges through it joyfully, dragging me after, and on all sides finding little surprises that he leaps upon like objects he has mislaid and expected never to find again. He brings me birds eggs, holding them gently cupped in his hand, pointing out the speckles and making little cries to tell me which bird it is. And occasionally, out of a clutch of six or seven, he will give me one to suck, pushing a grass stalk through each end and showing me how to draw the goodness out. He gives me seeds to eat, and straws to munch on. He finds roots that are sweet, and tubers, digging them up with his nails and cleaning them off with a thumb to make them ready for me to chew and swallow when I can, demonstrating, with his strong teeth, how they can be stripped and pounded to a pulp and the stringy fibers rejected. He finds a kind of mallow with a drop of honey in the horn, and holds his head back, pointing his tongue to take the single sticky dollop of it, and laughs when I try to do the same. His eyes are everywhere, as we walk, for whatever is edible and will sustain us.

The days pass, and I cease to count them. The river is far behind us.

Occasionally, far-off on one of the hilltops, we see horsemen, and watch the grasses part and darken as they ride downhill—towards what? We never know. Nor do we ever see anyone closer.

Once or twice in the night I wake to find the Child sitting stark upright beside me, listening. I hear nothing, but know what it is. There are wolves close by. When one of them approaches he rises softly, stands tall in the dark, and makes little growling sounds in his throat, and I see the wolf's eyes flash greenish as it lopes away.

I no longer ask myself where we are making for. The notion of a destination no longer seems necessary to me. It has been swallowed up in the immensity of this landscape, as the days have been swallowed up by the sense I now have of a life that stretches beyond the limits of measureable time. Is this what the shaman experiences when he sets off from the circle he has drawn with his own hand, and where his body squats? —this venturing out into a space that has no physical dimensions, and into a time that may be, in human terms, just a few minutes but is also eternity. Is this the land his spirit passes over on its way towards the pole? And is that what lies on the far side of this grassy plain? The pole? Is that where we are going, the Child and I? How long does it take to get there? In whose trance am I making this journey? And who is my companion?

I ask myself that now, watching him move in the

light just a few feet from me, naked, as he has been all these last days, poised in the stillness, half rising on one foot with his whole body alert to whatever it is that is in the grass beyond—who is he, this Child who leads me deeper into the earth, further from the far, safe place where I began, the green lands of my father's farm, further from the last inhabited outpost of the known world, further from speech even, into the sighing grasslands that are silence? Where has he come from? Out of which life? Out of which time? Did I really discover him out there in the pinewoods, or did he somehow discover me, or rediscover me, out of my own alienation from the world of men? Is he the Child of my first days under the olive trees at Sulmo? Is it the same Child? Is there, after all, only one? And where is he leading me, since I know at last that it is he who is the leader, he now who is inducting me into the mysteries of a world I have never for a moment understood. Wandering along together, wading through the high grasses side by side, is a kind of conversation that needs no tongue, a perfect interchange of perceptions, moods, questions, answers, that is as simple as the weather, is in fact the merest shifting of cloud shadows over a landscape or over the surface of a pool, as thoughts melt out of one mind into another, cloud and shadow, with none of the structures of formal speech. It is like talking to oneself. Like one side of the head passing thoughts across to the other, and knowing in a kind of foreglow, before the thought arrives, what it will be, having already received the shadow of its illumination.

I am growing bodiless. I am turning into the landscape. I feel myself sway and ripple. I feel myself expand upwards toward the blue roundness of the sky. Is that where we are going?

The earth, now that I am about to leave it, seems so close at last. I wake, and there, so enormous in their proximity to my eyeball that I might be staring through tree trunks into an unknown forest, are the roots of the grass, and between the roots, holding them together, feeding them, the myriad round grains of the earth, so minute, so visible, that I suddenly grasp the process by which their energy streams up through the golden stems. They are almost transparent, these fine long stalks. One can stare right through them and see the sap mounting in bubbles. They are columns of light, upright channels by which the earth feeds itself to the sky. And at their summit, so far-off they seem unreachable, the feathery grass heads plumping and nodding in the breeze, into whose sweet seeds all the richness of the earth ascends.

Round the base of these roots, seeking refuge amongst them as in a forest, finding food, are the smaller creatures—wood lice, ants, earwigs, earthworms, beetles, another world and another order of existence, crowded and busy about its endless process of creation and survival and death. We have come to join them. The earth's warmth under me, as I stretch out at night, is astonishing. It is like the warmth of another body that has absorbed the sun all day and now gives out again its store of heat. It is softer, darker than I could ever have believed, and when I take a handful of it and smell its extraordinary odors I know suddenly what it is I am composed of, as if the energy that is in this fistful of black soil had suddenly opened, between my body and it, as between it and the grass stalks, some corridor along which our common being flowed. I no longer fear it. I lie down to sleep, and wonder if, in the looseness of sleep, I mightn't strike down roots along all the length of my body, and as I enter the first dream, almost feel it begin to happen, feel my individual pores open to the individual grains of the earth, as the interchange begins. When I wake I am entirely reconciled to the process. I shall settle deep into the earth, deeper than I do in sleep, and will not be lost. We are continuous with earth in all the particles of our physical being, as in our breathing we are continuous with sky. Between our bodies and the world there is unity and commerce.

Perhaps that is why the breaking of the earth around us into the newness of spring seems, this time around, to be occurring at the very end of my nerves. The furriness of the little round catkins we discover on occasional bushes, the stickiness of new leaves that begin as a glossy finial and suddenly unfold out of themselves as tiny serrated heart shapes, all this, at such close range, seems miraculous, and so too is the exploding into the air of so many wings. A membrane strains and strains, growing transparent, till the creature who is stirring and waking in there is visible in all its parts, forcing its own envelope of being towards the breaking point till with its folded wings already secure in the knowledge of flight, and of all the motions of the air, it flutters free. The whole earth creaks and strains in the darkness. The sounds are tiny, but to an ear that has been laid close to the earth, entirely audible. I think sometimes that if I were to listen hard enough I would hear my own body breaking forth in the same way, pushing at the thin, transparent envelope that still contains it, that keeps it from bursting forth into whatever new form it has already conceived itself as being, something as different from what we know as the moth is from the chrysalis.

The Child too seems to me to have a new being out here, and I no longer ask myself what harm I may have done him. He too has survived his season among men. Some new energy is in him. He is lighter. He moves faster over the earth. He is alert to every shift of the wind and mood of the sky as it carries the weather of tomorrow and the day after towards us, to every scent of the hundred grasses and herbs and fat little buds that spread around us their invisible particles. It is these grasses and their parasites, the worms, the grubs, the small winged grasshoppers, that provide us with nourishment. The Child gathers them where they hang, feeding in their chains above the earth, one creature grazing, taking in goodness, and passing on into another's mouth. We are at the end of the chain. Each day early, the Child hunts, feeding me now out of his world as I once fed him out of ours.

I watch him standing, at dusk, at the edge of whatever place we have found to rest for the night, staring out northward into the immensity of grass.

Does he know what lies out there? Is he returning to some known place, and leading me there? Each day now I have less and less strength to push on towards whatever goal it is—unannounced yet, among the miles

148

of grass—that we are headed for. Does he know where he is taking us? I feel his impatience to be moving, even as he stands at dusk, perfectly still against the reddening sky, casting his eye forward to where we will be, at the crest of that further rise, at this time tomorrow night. I watch him, and wonder what it is in his mind that gives our journey purpose. His whole body strains toward some distance that I cannot grasp from where I lie in the shade. He is full of it, of some suppressed passion for the furthest reaches of what he can see, and I feel that, glowing in him, as he stoops to bring me whatever he has found for us to eat, patiently sorting seeds for me, or showing me how to tackle water snails, or squeezing drops of water out of a piece of rag to wet my lips. He seems closer now than I ever thought possible. In those early days it seemed inconceivable that he should discover in himself this tender kinship with men that is visible now in every moment of his concern for me.

And yet for all this closeness, he seems more and more to belong to a world that lies utterly beyond me, and beyond my human imagining.

It is as if he moved simultaneously in two separate worlds. I watch him kneel at one of his humble tasks, feeding me, or cleaning up my old man's mess. And at the same time when I look up, he is standing feet away, as when I first saw him in the pinewood, a slight, incandescent figure, naked against the dusk, already moving away from me in his mind, already straining forward to whatever life it is that lies out there beyond our moment together, some life I have not taken into account, and which he will be free to enter only when our journey together is done. I have tried to induce out of the animal in him some notion of what it is to be human. I wonder now if he hasn't already begun to discover in himself some further being. Is he, in fact, as the villagers thought (their view was always simpler than mine, and perhaps therefore nearer the truth) some foundling of the gods? Is it his own nature as a god that his body is straining towards, at this edge of his own life where any ordinary child might be about to burst into manhood, and into his perfect limits as man? He moves out of sight, hovering there, vague and glowing, just beyond the capacity of my eye to distinguish what it sees. And at the same time, with bent back, he squats on his haunches, his grimy hands with their cracked and broken nails working to prepare the food I can barely swallow now. He takes infinite pains over it, half chewing the fibrous tubers to make them palatable and feeding me the pulp, as he must have seen animals do with their young.

And so we come to it, the place. I have taken my last step, though he does not know it yet, as he moves away as usual to forage for our evening meal. From here I ascend, or lower myself, grain by grain, into the hands of the gods. It is the place I dreamed of so often, back there in Tomis, but could never find in all my wanderings in sleep—the point on the earth's surface where I disappear.

It is not at all as I had imagined. There are no wolves. It is clear sunlight, at the end of a day like each of the others we have spent out here, a fine warm spring day with larks in the air, and insects shrilling under our feet. The Child is here. I watch him moving away along the edge of a stream, stooping, kneeling, starting off again with his spring-heeled gait as he gathers snails amongst the weeds.

Strange to look back on the enormous landscape we have struggled across all these weeks, across the sea, across my life in Rome, across my childhood, to observe how clearly the footprints lead to this place and no other. They shine in my head, all those steps. I can, in my mind, follow them back, feeling myself with each step restored, diminished, till I come to the ground of my earliest memories again, and am standing in the checkered light of olives at the very edge of our farm, with wings glittering beyond the low stone wall and a goatherd dozing against one of the olives, his rough head tilted back and all the throat exposed, as if he had been dozing like that, just as I last remember him, for nearly sixty years. One of the goats, which is black, has just jerked up on to its hind legs to munch at a vine shoot. It is spring. It is summer. I am three years old. I am sixty.

The Child is there.

He turns for a moment to gaze at me across his shoulder, which is touched with sunlight, then stoops to gather another snail from the edge of the stream. He rises and goes on. The stream shakes out its light around his ankles as he wades deeper, then climbs on to a smooth stone and balances for a moment in the sun, leaps, leaps again, then wanders upstream on the other bank, which is gravel, every pebble of it, white, black, gray, picked out and glittering in the late sunlight as in a mosaic, where he pauses, gathers one, two, four snails, and with the stream rippling as he steps in and out of it, walks on, kicking at the gravel with his toes and lost for a moment in his own childlike pleasure at being free.

I might call to him. I have the voice for that. But do not. To call him back might be to miss the fullness of this moment as it is about to be revealed, and I want so much, at the very end here, to be open to all that it holds for me.

The fullness is in the Child's moving away from me, in his stepping so lightly, so joyfully, naked, into his own distance at last as he fades in and out of the dazzle of light off the water and stoops to gather—what? Pebbles? Is that what his eye is attracted by now, the grayest, most delicately veined of them? Or has he already forgotten all purpose, moving simply for the joy of it, wading deeper into the light and letting them fall from his hands, the living and edible snails that are no longer necessary to my life and may be left now to return to their own, the useless pebbles that where they strike the ground suddenly flare up as butterflies, whose bright wings rainbow the stream.

He is walking on the water's light. And as I watch, he takes the first step off it, moving slowly away now into the deepest distance, above the earth, above the water, on air.

It is summer. It is spring. I am immeasurably, unbearably happy. I am three years old. I am sixty. I am six.

I am there.

AFTERWORD: A NOTE ON SOURCES

We know very little about the life of Ovid, and it is this absence of fact that has made him useful as the central figure of my narrative and allowed me the liberty of free invention, since what I wanted to write was neither historical novel nor biography, but a fiction with its roots in possible event.

What we do know comes from the poet himself: the place and date of his birth, the death of a brother one year older than himself in early youth, and of course the famous exile—though we have no explanation of why it was imposed. Ovid is very much an actor, inclined to exaggerate for effect, so very little of what he tells us is reliable. I have used his poem of exile, *Tristia,* for my picture of Tomis and have drawn on Book III of *Fasti,* his study of the chief Roman festivals, for details of the Parilia. My hint for the Scythian graves is in Herodotus.

The encounter with the Child, which makes up the main part of this book, has no basis in fact, but I have verified my description from the best account we have of such a phenomenon, J.M.G. Itard's painstaking observations of Victor, the wild boy of Aveyron, which no writer on the subject can ignore. Itard's involvement is that of the teacher, and growing as it does out of the eighteenth century, his interest is chiefly in the problems of innate and learned experience. It was partly to break into a field of more open possibilities that I set my narrative in a remote place about which almost nothing is known, and in an age, the dawn of the Christian era, in which mysterious forces were felt to be at work and thinking had not yet settled into a rational mode.

At a time when the Roman period had been sunk for nearly a thousand years in impenetrable obscurity, Ovid became a popular figure of mythology and the search for his grave resulted in the veneration of several legendary but spurious sites, some of them as far from his original place of exile as central Hungary. The actual date of his death, and its cause, remains mysterious.

To the Renaissance reader Ovid was the most modern of the Latin poets, the most worldly and accessible, the most human, his skepticism balanced by a love of the fabulous, the excessive. It is this modern quality I have tried to recreate, though the fate I have alloted him, beyond the mere fact of his relegation to Tomis, is one that would have surprised the real poet, since it attributes to him a capacity for belief that is nowhere to be found in his own writings. But that is exactly the point. My purpose was to make this glib fabulist of "the changes" live out in reality what had been, in his previous existence, merely the occasion for dazzling literary display.